Here in the World

✦

HERE IN THE WORLD

Victoria Lancelotta

COUNTERPOINT

Washington, D.C.

Library of Congress Cataloging-in-Publication Data
Lancelotta, Victoria, 1969–
Here in the world / by Victoria Lancelotta.
        p.   cm.
ISBN 1-58243-009-3 (alk. paper)
1. Southern States—Social life and customs—Fiction.
2. Single women—Fiction.   I. Title.
PS3562.A4669 H4 2000
813'.6—dc21   00-035890

FIRST PRINTING

Design and composition by Wilsted & Taylor
Jacket design by Wesley Tanner

COUNTERPOINT
P.O. Box 65793
Washington, D.C. 20035-5793

Counterpoint is a member of the Perseus Books Group

10   9   8   7   6   5   4   3   2   1

✦

C O N T E N T S

✦

ACKNOWLEDGMENTS

"In Bars," *Puerto del Sol*, Spring/Summer 2000. "The Guide," *Yellow Silk II* (Warner Books), 2000. "Festival," *Blue Cathedral* (Red Hen Press), 2000. "Here in the World," *Beloit Fiction Journal*, Spring 1999. "Spice," *Glimmer Train*, Fall 1999. "In Houses," Literal Latte, May/ June 1999. "Nice Girl," *The Ohio Review*, Spring 1998. "The Gift," *The Cream City Review*, Spring 1997. "Festival," *Mississippi Review Web*, September 1996. "The Guide," *Mississippi Review Web*, March 1996. "What I Know," *The Threepenny Review*, Summer 1995. "Quiet," *The Texas Review*, Fall/Winter 1994. "Full," *The Black Warrior Review*, Fall/ Winter 1994.

THE GUIDE

Listen. Here is a love story.

We filed to the altar in doll-sized veils and patent leather shoes, heads bowed, our trembling hands folded and held chest-high, and before kneeling to receive the wafer from the priest we approached the marble statue, genuflected, crossed ourselves in penance for the sins we would commit, and kissed the cold stone foot of Christ.

The pristine foot, worn smooth by lips like mine—the first man besides my father I had ever kissed. On my knees on the floor before it, the other girls behind me waiting for their turns. We knelt at the altar in our white dresses, a row of us on our knees, small cannibals, veiled heads thrown back, throats taut, tongues out, waiting for the priest to place the wafers in our mouths.

We were not to bite them, the nuns had told us that. The host was placed on the tongue and allowed to melt there, to dissolve. If we had bitten them, splintered the wafers between our small teeth, chewed them as we chewed everything else, I imagined they would explode in blood, fill our mouths with it, with the taste I knew from pulling out a loosened tooth, from sucking at a skinned knee—my body's betrayal of me.

Afterward, my mother boxed the dress and shoes. *I'll keep these for you,* she said, *for when you have a daughter of your own.*

✦   ✦   ✦

I am not a mother. I have never wanted that. My lover is a blind man whom I watched for days, for weeks, sitting at the bus stop bench outside my window, or else in the small park at the end of my block. I watched him from my bedroom window. From there, I could see everything—the sidewalk, the corner store, the rowhouses across the street, and the bench on which he sat. He sat neatly, knees and feet together, heavy shoes laced tight, his stick against his thigh. I watched him first from my window and then from the front steps, coming closer every week until I sat some few feet away from him at the far edge of his bench. He heard me sit, turned to me, and smiled. He reached his soft hand out and spoke.

He is older than he looks, that I know. His face is smooth, unlined. His hair is the black of crow's feathers. His eyes are blue and cloudy; they roll behind the glasses, drifting in slow orbits. I had never seen blind eyes before. That first day I walked him down the street, slowly, more slowly than he was used to walking, I think. I navigated curbs for him, the cracked and ruined sidewalk, the trash blown in his steps. I watched the people watch us. They smiled at me because I held his arm. They thought me kind, generous, but that was not the truth, not then, not now. There is nothing generous in me. I am greedy for him, gluttonous: I would fill myself with him, blind myself with him.

When we get home I bathe him. I take the clothes he peels off. I run his water hot. I kneel on the tile and soap the smooth unscarred expanse of him. He is mine to claim, to own: the soft whiteness of his flesh about to go to fat from the food I cook and serve him. I have no need of children.

When we are through I dry him off and lead him to my bed.

He likes best to make love to me in the daylight. He tells me to snap up the blinds. My windows face to other windows. He sits up in my bed, the glasses off, his eyes like spinning marbles.

Strip for me, he says. *I want to watch you strip.* He smiles at me, at where I stand, and I can see his gleaming teeth, his lips.

Move in front of the window, strip there, he says. *I want everyone to see you.*

He smiles like a dog, mouth stretched wide, his fingers spread out on the sheets to either side of him. His eyes won't stop their drifting.

There is no sound, now, no sound in the room at all, only the noise of traffic from the street. He is listening and hearing only this, and the beating of my heart is loud. My dress is damp from his bath and I have nothing on beneath it. I pull it over my head and toss it at his feet.

Come here, he says, leaning up and reaching for the dress, hooking it with his clawed fingers, crumpling the fabric.

+   +   +

He cannot see what he has done to me. My thighs and my hips are bruised and bitten until the blood rushes up beneath the skin, purple then yellow and gray, blotched and welted, as though I have taken to myself with a hairbrush, nothing like the neat marks the nuns left on the backs of my hands.

Who taught you how to eat? the nuns said to me at lunchtime. *If you're going to eat like that it's better not to eat at all,* they said, and swooped down on me like birds to carrion, taking my food away. *Come with us,* they said, and took me to stand over one of the other girls, a girl with a napkin in her lap and her sandwich cut in triangles. She ate the corners first, her face working like a rabbit.

She would be caught one day, crushed, I thought, flattened, bloodied, her unborn children dying with her.

There, the nuns said, leading me back to my chair, *that is how you eat.*

I remember the things they taught me, the ways to eat, to walk, to kneel and pray. *Humility,* they said, *modesty,* and the move from that to shame. I remember my hands clasped in my lap and my knees pressed tight together. *Cover yourself,* they said, *that body is not yours to give, that flesh is weak and stupid.* Not mine? I thought. Then whose?

The nuns were safe, I knew that then, their faces small pale moons, their bodies only memories, shrouded early for the grave. They had no need of penance, but I remember mine: the hot box of the confessional, the mimicked crucifixion, the words that stuck in my throat like bones—I have done *this*, and *this*. I knelt on scabbed knees and prayed not to cry.

THE GUIDE

The nuns told me of their pilgrimages to Fatima and Lourdes. They said they crawled across rocks and cobblestones until they bled, praying for the sick to be healed. My falls from bikes and swings, my scrapes and bruises, my paper cuts—*those are your gifts to God,* they said, *your little crosses.*

I learned how not to speak, how not to ask for what I should not have. I kept my prayers short, and I kept my secrets, rooted in my throat, blooming there, choking me with a rank and tangled garden of wishes: not to be thankful for my bruises and cuts, not to be on my knees, to be, please God, nothing like them, those women who were the walking dead.

I had imagined that I would forget these things, and sometimes I do. I have become neat, scrupulous in organization. My lover knows the placement of my furniture. It did not take him long. He moves through rooms easily, with more grace than I have ever had. But all this depends on me. If I leave a coat, a shoe, some newspaper on the floor after I've read to him, his balance will be thrown, and he will fall.

+ ✦ +

The corner store is where I go for food. I pull my dress back on and leave my lover in the bedroom. I move a chair for him to the window where he likes to sit, and I leave him. From the street I can see his face—from this distance, his glasses off, he looks like anyone else.

In the store, I move through the narrow aisles, brushing up against displays, knocking into stacks of cans. I always pick up what I drop. If something breaks I stop—I would never just walk past, pretending it wasn't me, or push a mess I've made beneath the ledge of the bottom shelf. I have learned to be honest.

The man at the counter undercharges me and I am quick to point this out. *Don't worry,* he says to me, smiling, *I have enough of your money.* He watches me leave with my bags, and though I say that I am honest there is still one thing—he doesn't know that I wear nothing underneath my dress but the crescents of dried blood a blind man's nails have gouged, moon-shaped on my thighs.

I could drop my bags in the doorway of the store and lift my skirt. Look at me, I could say, look at what he's done to me, at what I have let him do.

Do you have a daughter, I could say, can you imagine this on her?

If I opened my mouth to speak these things my throat would fill with the dirt of years and spill out of me, clots of it from between my lips.

My honesty has its limits.

No one sees these marks but me, and no one sees the things I do for him. I comb his hair, I clip his nails, his fingers wide and grasping, fat antennae; I would not be surprised to see eyes bloom at the tips. His toes are blunt stubs, as though they had been sawed off and sanded down, white in the heavy black shoes. With the clippers I prune tiny shards of him. *Not too short*, he says, *remember.*

When I leave the grocery he is still at the window, his head slowly moving, left to right, dipping at the sounds of horns and shouting children, swiveling and stopping short. There is no mistaking him now for someone fine.

He sits at the table while I prepare the food. Although he does not use his stick inside he has it now, and as I move from stove to sink he taps it across the floor, catching my ankles as I walk, or running it up my leg and under the skirt of my dress, rubbing between my thighs.

Hurry, he says, *I'm hungry.*

My lover eats with precision, with the exacting elegance of the blind. I set his plate before him and call for him the times of his food: meat at four o'clock, greens at eight, potatoes square on twelve. He keeps the fork in his left hand, knife in his right, rarely switching, never dropping. His quick neatness is astonishing. He cuts like a surgeon.

Across from him, my legs are spread, my skirt bunched, the skin of my thighs sticking to the seat of my chair. My elbows are on the table, the trash can is at my side, almost full with sodden newspapers, crusts of bread, coffee grinds, and ashes. I lift the meat with my fingers and gnaw around the bone, grease smeared across my face. The bits of fat and gristle I spit back out, directly into the trash can. They raise little clouds of ash.

The blind man sits, still cutting. His hands are deadly accurate.

I lower my face to the plate in front of me, smear it in the food. He could lick me clean.

Who taught you how to eat? I would ask him, but I know better than that.

He serves himself carefully from the bowls at the center of the table, and I watch him, mime him. My plate is covered with food that I don't want, a wreck of it, dripping over the edges of the china.

It was good, he says, and pushes back his chair, reaches for his stick. He moves off to the bedroom. I scrape the food into the trash, drop the silverware on top of it, the plates, the serving bowls. I wipe my face on my skirt and my hands on my legs and go into the bedroom.

He lies in the near-dark, his shoulders propped by pillows. I stand at the foot of the bed and strip, invisible, and wonder how he dreams of me, in what strange language of flesh and scent and voice. He has never seen my face, or the color of my hair, but he tells me he loves my body and to him I am only that, skin and muscle and strong bone. When I wind myself around him his hands grope and search for the things he cannot see, and he tells me that I am a secret to everyone but him.

Where are you, he says, *what are you doing?* I stand motionless by the bed. I have no violence in me. I would never take his stick and hide it. I would not strike him, mark him with the print of my hand. I would not take his food away or run a bath too hot.

Listen, I say to him, *can you hear me?* and I begin to move, to dance, naked in front of him, and he cannot see what there is for him to take. My legs are long and slicked with grease, my hair is damp with sweat. No man has seen me stripped, no one has seen me move like this, and I have nothing to confess.

Dance with me, I say, *get up,* and reach my hand out for him, moving it just beyond his reach each time he leans to take it. I know more games than he does, I know them better. I dance around the bed, spinning, moving backwards, scuffing my bare feet on the carpet, a noise that he can follow——I am fair if nothing else.

He moves from the bed, hands outstretched, and lunges for me, but he is too slow, too heavy, his foot tangled in the sheet, and I watch him fall.

Dance with me, I say again, leaning naked over him, a spill of sightless flesh on my bedroom floor. My hair brushes his face, and he grabs for that but I am too quick for him.

I have never felt so light, my body has never worked so well as this. The blind man is on his hands and knees, he is crawling towards my voice. I crook a finger he cannot see, I cock a hip, I pose. There is nothing I would not do for him.

A little more, a little farther, I say, *a little to the left.*

Over here.

I step first on my toes and then my heels, I feint, I dip, I back around a chair, holding it between us. I think, there is no end to the things we do, the care we take.

That will be your job, the nuns said, *when you have children of your own. You will teach them to be meek, to suffer things in silence.*

But there is no meekness left in me, I have spit it out. I am empty, clean, waiting to be filled. The feel of my own skin is soft, softer than I knew, and my balance is perfect——my feet, my legs, the rocking of my hips, the swaying of my breasts.

I move around the chair. I prod his smooth chin with my foot.

Look at me, I say, prodding, amazed at the reach of my leg. I tilt his face up to me and he rises to his knees, unsteady in his love, his sweet mouth working, mouthing words I can't make out: the stupid chant of litany, of prayers long unanswered for things he cannot have. What could a blind man pray for, what thing that he would get?

WHAT I KNOW

This is the sort of air that sticks, the kind you want to pull off you, away from your skin, or wipe away in great sluicing motions and back into the water where it surely belongs, because this is not the sort of air that anyone could breathe. You could die, drown, trying to breathe this. To have anyone touch you would be unbearable.

This is a thing I know: the breeze that comes from the water is a hot one, heavy with the smells of fish and oil, and it leaves a warm sticky film on your lips and skin. I know that the people who laugh and drink on the boats anchored here for the night must be lying: it is no different where they are than where I walk along the dock. The air is no better for them, and I have no breath to laugh.

+ + +

Jerry is sick. He thinks that he is dying. He has thought this since coming home, back from wherever he was. He sits in his bedroom, on the third floor of a row house on Aliceanna

Street, and talks about whom he will give his belongings to. He sits on his bed by the window where there is no screen and picks leaves off the tree that the neighborhood association planted. They dug up a square of sidewalk to do it. The leaves are small, pale green with crumbling brown edges. They look tired.

"Margaret can have the couch," he says, shredding. His fingers are long and vaguely blue in the streetlight that shines through the window; they tear a leaf carefully, according to the veins. "And I think Bob should get the stereo." There is a small mound of green on the sheet in front of him.

✦   ✦   ✦

From Jerry's house I walk to the pharmacy, a mile down Aliceanna Street and up Broadway two blocks to Eastern. The walk is not entirely safe, but it is too hot for trouble. On Aliceanna Street boys sit on their front steps with their girlfriends and babies, the doors behind them open. You can see into their living rooms if the lights are on, a bare bulb in the ceiling or sometimes just the blue flickering of a TV. The girls wear shorts and dirty bedroom slippers. The boys are shirtless and barefoot. Sometimes there is a naked child with wet sticky hair in the doorway, crying. The babies sit on their mothers' laps, or their grandmothers'.

I know about these families, their houses that are too hot for them, the kitchen air thick with cooking and grease. I know about the women, grandmothers at thirty-five, with cracked hands and dyed hair, women who will cuff their daughters if they don't answer a baby's cry. When the sun goes down they take off their aprons and come outside, out onto the white marble steps or lawn chairs on the sidewalk. They come outside to smoke and drink beer, to call the children out of the dark street. It is too hot. They are too tired to sleep.

In the pharmacy I pick up antibiotics and aspirin and a bottle of green shampoo. Jerry did not ask for the shampoo, but there was none in the bathroom. I pay with money he's given me.

I am a nurse, a maid: a nursemaid. He would not eat if I did not bring him food, although sometimes if I am busy I call Cheryl and ask her to take him a salad, anything. Anything extra from her kitchen, I say, and tell Jerry I will be over later. Cheryl, and Margaret and Bob, all of them, come once a week, once every ten days. I am there every night since Jerry's been home.

I walk the long way back with my bag from the pharmacy, past the bars on Broadway and through the crowds on the sidewalk. They come out in this heat, thinking it will be cooler at night, by the water. Women in white dresses, sandals and pearls, men in fancy linen shorts and huaraches. The men guide the women through doorways with a hand, light on the small of a back. Their clothes will crumple in the heat of the bars.

It is quieter by the water, darker. There are no bars along this street, no houses, just the brick facades of warehouses, the small shadows of stray dogs, and sometimes rats. They are large, the rats. I imagine them to be slippery. Children scream from a few blocks over.

Jerry has not moved, it seems: the pile of shredded leaves on the bed is larger. He does not turn to look at me when I come in.

"Maybe you should take the stereo," he says, his voice drifting out the window, soft, lost in the leaves still left on the tree.

"Jerry." I put the bag down. There are wet marks on the paper from where I held it. My skin is sticky. If I could, I would peel myself out of it and hang it on the shower rod to dry.

"No, I want to be fair. Everyone should get what they most deserve. You'll take my bed."

"Here's your medicine, Jerry. I'm going to run you a bath."

"I don't want to take a bath," he says. He turns to look at me, his face backlit from the streetlight. The ends of his blonde hair are silver in the light, his mouth dark and sagging.

"You smell," I say, slowly, but from where I stand I can only smell my own sweat, rank and sweet. "I'm running you a bath."

His bathroom is clean, barely used since he came back. We were on the roof over a month ago, the soles of our shoes sinking into the baking tar. *If you don't stay with me,* he'd said, *I'll leave. I'll leave and I won't come back.*

I go back to the bedroom and get him. I get the green shampoo.

"It's too bright in here," he says when he is in the tub. He pulls the blinds and sleeps during the day, sits in the dark by the window at night. His skin was sunburned, blistered, when he came back.

"When I was gone," he says, "everyone I met said how crazy I was to live so close to D.C. What if there's a war? A bomb? We'll all fry,"

"There's no war," I say, pouring water from a plastic cup over his head, "and we're frying now."

"It's not safe here, Rebecca."

"You're not dying, you're just sick. You're not taking care of yourself and God knows what germs you picked up on the road. But you're not going to die."

"Would you cry if I did?"

His back and chest have peeled and scarred. There are new wrinkles around his eyes. He has told no one where he went, though he hints that it was Mexico. The bath water is cloudy with shampoo. I stand and give him a towel.

"There's bread and cheese downstairs. I want to take a shower now."

"No, don't."

"What? Jerry, I'm soaked. I'm filthy."

"Don't," he says. "I want to be able to smell you."

✦ ✦ ✦

When I was a little girl I played hopscotch in the alley behind my grandparents' house, less than a mile from here. The alley was safer than the street, my grandmother said, and I played barefoot until I had to go to the hospital for a tetanus shot. I'd stepped on a pull-tab.

Tonight the boys are using Jerry's front steps as home base for their game, I'm not sure what it is. They run, pounding on the hoods of cars until voices from the other houses scream at them to stop it now, right now. They wipe the sweat from their faces with their shirts, or pull the shirts off and whip each other with them. These boys tonight are magic, or something close. They run screaming through the heavy air as though it doesn't touch them, they shake the sweat from their hair like ponies, like dogs, and I shrink back, helpless in the doorway.

✦   ✦   ✦

Up the dark stairs Jerry is lying in bed, the sheet wadded around his waist, his hair damp and curled from the bath. With his thin chest, his ribs and scars, he looks like a saint, like the crucified Jesus that hung in my grandmother's kitchen.

"You didn't eat," I say.

"You didn't shower."

"Jerry, you have to eat."

"I'm not hungry." He pushes the sheet down so I can see him, the shadowed hollow of his hips. I think of my grandmother: *Clean your plate, there are children starving somewhere, anywhere.*

"Will you come to bed?"

I sit on the edge of the bed and he lays his hand on my back. I can feel the dry heat of it through my shirt. He does not sweat, not that I've seen, and yet the sheets smell faintly of sickness, of age. His hand will leave a smoking hole in my flesh. I shift on the bed, away from him.

"Rebecca—"

"I'm taking a shower now."

He sighs, rolls over, rests his chin on the window sill.

+   ✦   +

There is a cotton dress of mine still in the closet that I put on after the shower. In the bathroom ceiling is an open skylight that leads to the roof. A wooden ladder that Jerry built is mounted on the wall. I climb up with my towel around my neck.

The breeze on the roof is cooler than any I've felt tonight, but the tar is still soft; it would steam if it rained. I spread the damp towel out before I sit. Jerry and I slept here. We brought pillows and a quilt to lie on and a sheet to cover us, a bucket of ice to rub on our necks. In the morning the sun burnt off the haze on the water. When I woke I would check to be sure we were still close to the middle of the roof: I had nightmares, sometimes, that I'd rolled over and off the edge, and in the dreams I would snatch at the thin branches of the tree, coming away with handfuls of twigs and leaves, and waking before I hit the sidewalk, or the hood of a car.

The boys are still out. They must be directly below me. Their shouts are close but from where I sit I can't see them. There is music now, too, thin and crackling, from a small radio in someone's living room, and also the sounds of a baseball game, the announcer excited, the crowd cheering, and this, I think, from the open door of the bar on the corner. But I can't see to be sure.

What I can see are the roofs of these row houses, sloping down towards the harbor like steps, and from here it seems that I could jump from one to the next, into the water at the end. There are lights on the water, reflected silver and red from the neon, the streetlights and shop lights, and across the water the sugar factory and steel mill, and the expressway: north to New York and south, far, I'm not sure how far. The lights stretch on all sides.

I could go down into this dark house and bring Jerry up here to sleep, where there is some air to breathe, but his bed is soft, and even on a quilt now his bones would clack against the roof, the knobs of his spine and the ridges of his hips, a hollow, knocking sound. I would wake to find his long blue fingers circling my wrist, light, but with all the hot force of what he knows: that he is dying, that it is his right not to believe me when I tell him otherwise.

It is late, now, probably close to midnight, and I stretch on my belly across the roof, hold tight to the rain gutter and look over the side. I am cautious. At night I am sure to lock my windows and doors. I know there are not many safe places— this, for instance, is certainly not one. But on this block the doors of the houses are open, most of the lights still on, shadows moving in the narrow front hallways. I know that these open doors are not invitations, that there are dark bedrooms above them where people are deciding that perhaps they can sleep now, stretched naked on hot rough sheets, wet in the creases of their chins, in the hollows of their throats. They will shout downstairs for the radios to be turned off, the front doors closed and locked.

The boys are scattering. They have put their shirts back on, and they punch and shove each other, laughing, before moving off towards home, their faces wet, shining. Below me Jerry coughs, a small sound, and I can see the branches of the tree shake slightly, a few leaves dropping to the sidewalk. Sooner or later he will get up to eat. He will eat secretly, hungrily, not letting anyone know; he will talk about who will get the refrigerator.

Two men come out of the bar on the corner. They shout goodnights to the people inside. Their voices are loud. They stumble on the sidewalk and speak of rain. One of them looks up, straining, searching the dark sky for clouds that are not there. He scans the rooftops, and for an instant I think his eyes meet mine, his small glittering eyes, and perhaps they do, but his gaze passes over me without pause or surprise. There might be no one up here at all.

QUIET

This is how it started: when Jane was fourteen she was kissed by a boy named Peter. They were in a muddy field at night, in March, and the grass was crushed wet with dew and spilled beer. They had moved off away from the rest of the party, almost to where the field ended and the woods began, and Peter put his hands on her back and his tongue in her mouth. She was unsure of what to do, exactly, but thought that since his hands were on her back she should do the same with him, and she also moved them around, her hands, over his shoulders and down to his belt, and tried to remember to move her tongue around as well. It was, she thought, a lot to keep track of.

When they were finished kissing, they moved back into the circle of the party, and Peter stayed at her side, not touching her exactly but allowing his arm to brush her side, as if by accident. He offered her sips of his beer and he offered to walk her home. She thanked him but shook her head and ran alone through the neighbors' backyards and down the street.

When she got home she realized she was shivering, and that her shoes were soaked through, her feet chilled and wrinkled on the bottoms.

Jane did not try out for the cheerleading squad or the chorus or the drama club, nor did she stay in her room reading romance novels or watching old movies on TV. She spent her time with Audrey Gordon, who was three inches taller and had big breasts. When they went out together the boys would look at Audrey first, always, on account of the breasts, but Audrey was clumsy and she laughed too often, or too soon. Jane watched her: she watched her stick her poor stupid tits in the boys' faces and stare at their knees, or the floor, and laugh at nothing funny. The boys, then, would roll their eyes at one another and walk away, and Audrey would look at Jane, defeated.

It was important, Jane thought, that even if the boys did not pay particular attention to her, they did not laugh at her either.

+   +   +

Jane decided that she hated her face. When she was younger she hadn't paid any attention to it, or to her clothes. She would walk by mirrors and not notice a shirttail out or hair that needed combing. But after Peter, after the boys who stared at Audrey, she would sit in front of the mirror in her bedroom with the freshman class book in her lap. She would flip through the pages and stare at herself, then flip and stare some more. Her face, she thought, just didn't fit: the angles and shadows under her eyes and cheekbones next to the other girls, their smiles and dimples. She looked like a foreigner, strange.

She took Audrey to the mall with her one afternoon and waited in the department store for a free makeover. When her turn came she sat on the stool and waited to look different, older, to look like the popular girls at school, like the girls in the magazines.

The woman working took Jane's face in her hands and turned it from left to right. "Honey," she said, "I'll give you just a little color now but come back in a few years and we'll do you up right." She picked up her brushes and leaned in close. She smelled like mint and perfume. "When you're older," she said softly, "you will be beautiful. You'll grow into that face, honey, trust me."

Jane, before leaving, bought an eyeliner and two lipsticks, and with the change from that a pack of cigarettes from a vending machine in a restaurant. She stuffed the bags into her purse and stood with Audrey outside the mall, chewing gum, waiting for her mother to pick them up.

+   ✦   +

It occurred to Jane to wonder why Peter had not spoken to her at school after he kissed her. She watched him, casually, and she was not upset about it, but interested, interested in the way this whole thing worked with boys. Peter was not nasty, but he never said more than *Hello, how are you,* and then the same to Audrey, before walking by them. Audrey would get ready to laugh, but Peter was gone before she could.

There were times when Audrey would ask Jane what she thought was wrong, why at parties no boys came to her. Jane thought she knew, some of it if not everything. She knew that Audrey got nervous so that her hands would sweat, and she would wipe them on her pants over and over until her palms were red and chapped, and the boys noticed that, and some thought she might have a skin disease. She knew also that Audrey was afraid, afraid of getting in trouble with her parents and so would only pretend to drink. But also she was afraid of what would happen if a boy did pay attention, too much maybe. What would she do then, if one came too close or touched her too long?

Aside from all this, though, Jane knew that Audrey had the tits, and the face, a face prettier than her own, and if she couldn't figure out what to do past that it was not, Jane thought, her problem. So when Audrey asked what was wrong Jane would shrug and smile and say, *I don't have a boyfriend either, do I?*

And she didn't; for a long time after Peter kissed her she was quiet. She sat in the corner of the cafeteria at school so she could see the whole room, the big tables with groups sitting and laughing and the smaller ones along the sides, tables for two where couples sat and the boys would sometimes feed their girls ice cream or spaghetti. She went to the parties and stood in the shadows and watched the boys with their arms around the girls' shoulders or around their waists, proprietary. And the girls were laughing, but serious also, Jane thought, because this was serious business. She would leave the parties early, before her parents expected her home, and sit in the living room and talk with them about her friends who were the children of their friends. They sometimes drank tea, and when her parents went to bed she went to her room but did not sleep. She closed her door and put a towel under it and opened the window, not much if it was cold out. She sat at the mirror and put makeup on—makeup that she never wore outside her room—and stared at her face. She stared until her reflection was out of focus, the lines blurry and the eyes wide, unmoving, until she imagined that even if she moved the face in the mirror would remain frozen.

She would blink rapidly until the face in the mirror was her own again and then, at the mirror by the window, she would smoke. Would practice smoking. She was getting good at it, she thought.

She would pitch the cigarette into the bushes below her window and wave her arms until the air was clear, then go to the bathroom to wash her face. After that, if she was sure her parents were asleep, she took the empty soda bottles from her closet and wrapped them in a towel so they wouldn't clink. She took them down to the liquor cabinet in the basement and poured carefully, clear liquids in one bottle, dark in the other, never too much at once, filling the soda bottles over days. If she was calm enough when she finished, if her hands weren't shaking, she would pour water into the bottles of gin and vodka. Her parents drank a lot. Her father's office was next to a liquor store and he got a discount when he bought in bulk.

Then she would go back upstairs, the bottles wrapped in the towel, and shove the towel with the bottles behind shoeboxes in her closet. She would get in bed, staring at the ceiling, waiting for her heart to slow. There were always sealed full bottles in the back of the cabinet downstairs—extra, for when company came—and she thought about these. She knew they were there and she thought that she would take one of those one day. She had not had a drink yet, not from her closet. She was waiting. She didn't know yet what for.

+   ✦   +

"Audrey, "Jane said, "get your brother to get us some beer."

"My brother's only eighteen."

"So? He's got an I.D., I bet. And if he doesn't one of his friends will."

"I don't know, Jane. I don't want to ask him, you know, if my mother finds out . . . ."

They were in Jane's bedroom, and Audrey was trying on Jane's clothes. When she took a shirt off it was stretched, the seams pulled crooked. Jane was sitting on the windowsill smoking. "You're stretching them," she said.

"Huh?"

"My shirts," Jane said. "You're stretching them. I'm going to have to run them in the dryer now."

"Oh. Sorry." Audrey put her own shirt back on and sat on the bed. "I don't know, Jane. About my brother. And anyway, why? Someone always has beer, it's not like you need it personally."

"I need it personally. Talk to your brother. Or I'll do it. Then if your mother finds out you won't have anything to do with it."

Audrey shrugged. She tucked her blouse in and stood. "Whatever. I have to go now anyway."

That night, Jane smoked two cigarettes before she got in bed. She turned out the light and pulled the blankets up. She thought of Audrey, probably playing cards with her mother in their kitchen, and of Peter, and of all the boys like him. She wondered if they'd noticed how quiet she had been, if they'd noticed the months of quiet and of watching, if they'd noticed her in the corners, and if they'd wondered why. She lay in bed and thought about the thing she was waiting for.

+   +   +

Jane did not have a party on her sixteenth birthday. Instead, she cut her hair short. When she left the salon she took her hair with her, a long braid of it, caught at both ends with pieces of ribbon. She hung it on her mirror.

"It's to remind me," she told Audrey.

"Of what?"

Jane could not answer.

+   +   +

They dressed for the last party before summer at Jane's house. The bedroom door was shut, the towel beneath it, and incense burned in a saucer. Jane tapped her ashes in the saucer.

"My parents think I'm getting high in here," she said. "I'm sure they think so but they're afraid to say anything to me. Funny, huh? I mean because I'm not."

She leaned close to the mirror with an eyeliner; she used it carefully. Audrey sat on the bed, picked at a thumbnail.

"What are you going to do about Ben?" Audrey asked, picking.

"What about Ben?" Careful not to move her face too much, leaning even closer to the mirror, penciling in her lips. She dragged on the cigarette and pitched it hard out the window. The ember flickered on the lawn and vanished.

"You know, he was asking about you."

"Oh. That. I'm going to fuck him."

Audrey blinked stupidly. "Jane——"

"What?" She sprayed her hair into disarray. "What? Well, you asked." She pulled her hair, strands of it, up and away from her strange face, and then other strands up from the nape of her neck. She went to the closet and took out a bottle of vodka.

"You're not really going to, are you?" Audrey said.

Jane drank from the bottle and put it on the dresser. She pulled her shirt low on her shoulders and sucked her stomach in, turning to the side. She shrugged her shoulders, shrugged her shirt down farther. She poked silver hoops through her ears.

"Yes," she said. "I'm really going to fuck him." She turned to Audrey, to her face and her tits that were even larger than they had been and seemed, to Jane, to be sagging a little already. Audrey's bra straps were thick; they showed through her white blouse.

"Jane—"

"For Christ's sake, Audrey, I'm kidding!" She pulled her hair and smoothed her shirt, pulled her jeans down lower on her hips, and she was all smooth shoulders and flat stomach, bare and white. She drank from the bottle again and grinned.

"Kidding," she said, "kidding. I mean, Audrey, do I look like I'm out to get fucked?"

+ ✦ +

The party that night was close enough for them to walk but they drove in Audrey's mother's car. There was beer in the car and Jane opened one and drank on the way. She smoked also and was careful to let the smoke go out the window. She played the radio.

Audrey parked the car down the block from the party behind a dozen or more other cars. Jane turned off the radio and finished her beer. The engine ticked. She heard music ahead.

"Another one," she said, motioning to Audrey. She checked her hair and lipstick in the mirror and drank the beer Audrey gave to her. She drank the beer and remembered what it was like to be quiet all the time.

She got out of the car and jumped up and down on the street as if she were cold. She finished the beer and threw the bottle into the gutter where it shattered. She turned to Audrey and winked in a nasty way.

"Liquid charm," she said. "You can't leave everything up to your tits."

And then Audrey was out of the car too, staring at her feet, tucking her blouse and checking her belt.

"Come on, move it," Jane said, staring up the street, wrapping her purse strap tight around her fingers as though she were going to hit someone with it.

"Let's go, let's go," she murmured, and they started down the street, Jane a half-stride ahead.

The best part of any party, Jane thought, was walking into it, the best part and the most serious part. She did not speak to anyone on the lawn. She dropped her cigarette on the doorstep and opened the door and stopped for a moment and exhaled the smoke as she stepped inside. She pushed her way straight through to where the beer was and drank a full bottle, stopping only once for breath, and then opened another bottle and lit a fresh cigarette.

Peter was there, and the boy named Ben, and others, and she let them speak to her—she felt strongly that this was what she was doing, *letting* them, and as she spoke to them her voice grew hoarse. She imagined what they were thinking there in the middle of the smoke and music: *I never noticed her, did she always go to school with us?* or *She has no tits, that's for sure* or *Didn't she used to sit in corners and not talk? Was that her, was that this one?*

She let Ben take her by the wrist and lead her to the back hallway. He pulled her to him and she let him kiss her and she wondered what Audrey was doing, where she was, who she was talking to, and Ben was pushing a door open and backing her up, still kissing her, and then he stopped kissing her and she opened her eyes and there was the bed and she was not surprised. She moved to the door and closed it behind them and then moved to the bed and sat, on the edge, in the dark.

Ben, she thought she said, and he was on her, pushing her flat, one hand on her bare belly. She opened her legs so he could press himself between them and she wondered how long it would take and he was pulling at her jeans, her tight jeans, and she wiggled her hips to squirm out of them so he could get a hand in her underpants. She reached for the waist-band but he slapped her hand away and ripped a bit of the elastic. Her shirt was still on and his pants were loose around his hips and he was inside her then like that and he did not stay for long, and she felt a burning after and sat up to brush her own hair back. She touched her ear and her fingers came away bloody from the earring that had been accidentally torn from the lobe.

+ ✦ +

Jane was home by twelve and in bed by twelve-thirty. She lay in bed with the windows open and heard, or thought she heard, the noise of the party, the last one before summer. She thought she would go to the park at nights during the summer with the others, with Ben maybe, or Peter or someone else, and they would drink beer and smoke cigarettes and throw Frisbees around. She thought they would have cars there and leave the doors open and play the radios loud. And when it got late she would get into one of the cars with Ben or Peter or someone else, and they would roll up the windows against

QUIET

the mosquitoes. She would be tanned, so dark in her clothes at night that she'd be almost invisible, only her breasts white under the boy's hands. She imagined being invisible. She lay in bed and thought of these things.

IN BARS

I'm good in bars. It's a talent, and don't let anyone tell you something different: the way to walk in, to sit, to sip a drink and smile slowly, to look so that when he sits down next to you, buys you another, leans into your perfume, he can't believe it, can't believe how blessed he is to be near an angel like you. Because an angel is what you are for that moment, in his eyes—he needs to be in your light. And the light in bars is forgiving.

In that light I can believe in the waiting, the chance of what might happen, might be said, be offered: a new voice, a small thing. I believe that whoever he is, he is just the same as I am—his flesh, his blood, his heart, the things he wants, the way he wants them, and how much. This is what we all hope for, and there are times when I can keep myself from knowing better.

There are nights when I am beautiful, when I catch myself in the mirror behind the bottles and can almost believe what

I see there. In those blinking lights like Christmas we're all beautiful, all of us, sitting in a row, children again, eager to please—we raise our hands for the bartender, just like that, raised hands and smiles.

I understand certain things. I understand what it is to be patient, and to wait. I understand that fear is the thing that will kill you, will choke you, will carve itself into your face like a hot blade and ruin it.

I am not afraid of waiting—I am not afraid and I am not in love. Love is what happens when someone sees himself in you, and that has never happened to me. But I am still looking.

✦   ✦   ✦

My house is a row house in the center of a block of them, tall and narrow and made of brick and Formstone. It is easy to hear what goes on in the houses to either side, especially in the summer, in the quiet of morning.

Mornings, I sit in my house and listen for the neighbors. They are Hugh and Kate, and they are beautiful—gold and roses, hair that I would like to touch. When they moved in they came knocking on my door, holding a plate of strawberry muffins, and when I think of them still, I think of sweet warm foods, what you might feed a child—cobbler, turnovers, fruit pies with cream. We have good fruit in the summer, even here in the city, pints of berries from the Arabers that still smell of dark soil, melons with juice like honey. Hugh and Kate are like that.

I wake and lie still, imagine them damp from showers, wrapped in white terry-cloth robes, with mugs of coffee, newspaper. I imagine this life going on next to mine.

The houses on this block are repetitive in their symmetry: bedroom to bedroom, kitchen to kitchen, the separation of a wall. I get out of bed and go barefoot, quiet down the stairs to the small room behind the kitchen where I keep the extras of things—paper towels, laundry soap, cleaning supplies, bags. On one wall is shelving that I put up, stacked with what you might have called a dowry in some other time or circumstance: my grandmother's linens, fine embroidery at the edges, bedding I have not unwrapped. I reach for a towel and hear Hugh on the other side of the wall—his breath, fast and hard, the clank of weights and barbells, grunts, and under my feet the vibration of the floor in time with all of this. I imagine I can smell his sweat beneath the ribboned sachets, the clean powdery scent of my own things.

That is how close I am to them.

+ ✦ +

In bars, the juice is canned, metallic, citrus gone rusty and old—screwdrivers, greyhounds, sea breezes—better to mix with sodas if you have to mix at all.

Vodka rocks, bourbon neat, and in between each a plain tonic with lemon. A good bartender notices this, notices your steady walk at closing time.

At a bar, the stools should be high but not too high—you don't want to have to slouch, not unless you mean to, unless you mean to lean in close, sway-backed and forward on the seat, shoulders pulled back and pretty, pointed upward on the spine. This is a thing I could tell Kate, a thing she does not need to know.

+ ✦ +

In my house, I have candlesticks and cloth napkins, got when I thought my life would be different than it is today. I have cookbooks, potholders. I have drawers full of lingerie that no one sees but me. I have things that I keep hidden—a set of keys, a pair of gloves, both from the same house, the same man. The keys were mine, the gloves his, borrowed, and when I left I told myself I'd return them both, that I didn't want to leave the door unbolted, and that my hands were cold. *When I see him again*, I thought. *Time for all this when I see him again*. These are the things you tell yourself, driving away from a place, to keep yourself from turning back.

But tonight Kate has invited me for dinner, a note tucked in my front door, blurred ink on heavy stationery. I am showered, I am prompt, I am bringing a bottle of wine, five feet from my steps to theirs. The air is soft, the sky still light. The boys on the corner of the block are nothing dangerous yet, the girls in their houses still safe.

"Celia," Kate says, opening the door, taking the wine from me and pulling me inside as though she has something to show me, something wonderful. "Hugh, look," she calls, "Celia brought wine!" She has the bottle in one hand, my wrist in the other, leading me back toward the kitchen. And what I see is that the house is perfect, not a packing box in sight, glass-topped tables and polished brass, a hat stand.

Hugh is standing at the stove, wooden spoon in hand. "Celia," he says, and nods, looking at Kate and the wine she has set on the table. "This sauce is ready." He turns, drops the spoon on the counter, splattering red, and opens a cabinet. "Sit down," he says, glancing at me over his shoulder, and there is the sound of glasses being gathered, rims pinched between his fingers. "Kate will have the food in a minute."

I sit at the table and Kate brings steaming plates, centers the salt and pepper. Hugh sets down glasses for each of us and takes up the wine, scanning the label before putting the bottle in the cabinet below the sink. He moves to the refrigerator and opens the door—a big man, like men are supposed to be—and draws out a pitcher of lemonade. He fills our glasses, then takes his plate to the stove, pushes half of his food back into the pot. Kate waits to sit until he does. Her feet just touch the floor.

When dinner is finished I send them off into the living room and insist on making the coffee. I stack dishes in their dishwasher and arrange cookies on a plate, line up china bowls of milk and sugar, with small spoons. I can hear them from where I stand in the kitchen, the rustling of Kate's skirt, Hugh's voice soft and pitched high, the sound of some small animal.

✦　✦　✦

My bedroom is small and uncluttered, manageable in its way. A wide window to my left, a bulletin board on the wall to my right where cards could be tacked. Every other surface is smooth, shining. Seven steps from wall to wall, window to door, a white box, me unwrapped in it. From my bed I can hear the clatter of dishes being put into cabinets and then steps up the stairs, a faucet running, the snick of a closet door. They are in their bedroom.

Get down, I hear, *down.*

Hugh, please—

Something heavy dropping, and outside, the slam of a car door.

Behave, Katie. Now.

I am lying in my bed, in my empty house, thinking of what to wish for: a slice of walnut cake, a new radio, a parakeet. Hair like Kate's to spread over my back, long hair like that, voices in my house. Blue lights flash by my window but there is no siren.

Down, Katie. Good girl. Good girl.

✦　　✦　　✦

In bars, I dance. I love that. That kind of sweat is different from any other, better, rising up from under the perfume of so many people—the scent of us, of what we wear beneath our clothes, of what our clothes are hiding, the scent of what we wish for. I dance with boys too young for me, close but never touching, their sweet smell almost too much for me to bear, or remember.

The truth is this: I am not so pretty, but there are times when I can forget this.

When the music stops I thank the boys, and some, the brave ones, will move to hug me, to catch me like a slippery fish, their faces rainbowed in the lights, and I breathe them in, my face in their necks, my throat filling with secrets they are too young to keep.

For that moment there is nothing for us to be afraid of.

✦ ✦ ✦

Three nights later the sun is down, the moon still pale, and through my open windows I can hear the summer slowing: the bell of the ice cream truck, the Arabers shouting, *corn 'n melons, corn 'n 'matoes*, the clop of their horses' hooves. Closer than all this is the knocking, Kate's voice floating up to me in my bedroom, and I run to let her in.

"I'm sorry," she says, "could I use your phone? Hugh cut the cords of ours. It's all right," she says, "he's passed out now."

Oh, I think, *oh*. I let her in, shut and lock the door.

"You can use the one upstairs," I say.

"Thank you." She moves to the couch and sits, folds her hands in her lap. "How much can you hear?" she says, her face small and round, doll-perfect, doll-smooth, and I am wondering what her hair would look like wet, how much darker it would be.

"Hugh—" I say, and she is young, so young, *How can she be so young*, I think, *and what will happen to me?*—"no," I say. "Hear what?"

"Never mind," she says, watching me, as though I might lie to her, and gets up from the couch and moves to the window.

"Doesn't it bother you," she says, "living here alone?"

Corn 'n melons, melons, 'matoes!

"No," I say and think of what is hidden in my house.

"I know what you must be thinking," she says, "but he's not usually like this. We don't usually drink. He doesn't, I mean. Not . . ." She wipes the flat of her hand down the length of her thigh, fists her skirt, a handful of flowered cotton. Her feet are bare. "Do you ever buy fruit from him?" she says, nodding toward the street outside my window, the cart piled with produce, women crowded around the back of it with brown bags of corn. She raises her hand to the sill and I can smell her, wine and something else beneath.

"You can shower here if you want," I say, "after you use the phone."

She turns back to me, slow on her bare feet. "The phone," she says, slowly, as though she has never heard of such a thing. "No. Thank you. I just—could I sleep? I could sleep for a few hours. I can't imagine it," she says, wiping at her skirt again, the fabric catching at her ring, "it seems so strange to buy food from someone like that, so dirty—it can't . . . it can't be *clean*."

I watch her and imagine what it would be like to live in her skin, her smooth pretty skin, to hear myself from the other side of that wall, to close my eyes and wake up in her bed, in her body, the bulk of her husband beside me, to touch him with her hands, eat him with her mouth—and me a ghost, an echo, a shadow puppet on the wall. It makes no difference that I don't know her, no difference at all. We are all the same. I stand in my house with the night coming on and imagine how, at her wedding, she must have danced.

✦   ✦   ✦

I take her upstairs to my bed, help her out of her clothes, bring a glass of water. The phone is on the night stand. She sleeps fast, the sheets kicked down, a shroud around her knees. She is not so tall as I am but softer; there are no angles to her body.

I understand that people will be kind if you let them, if you give them a reason to be. This is what we are waiting for, the patience we keep.

There are no sounds from the other side of the wall, and I think, *I will be happy someday. There is still time.*

She sleeps in my bed and there is a shifting in my body, a stroke of voodoo fingers, good medicine, good magic. I breathe her in, her smell like warming sugar, like caramel. I leave her there to sleep and take my keys and drive. The night is warm and close, and it is already true—I am happy.

✦   ✦   ✦

In bars, *possibility* becomes concrete, tangible with the power of faith. The air is thick with it. We all believe that we will leave somehow better than when we came, more real, more solid—that we will inhabit the world with a greater density, that someone will look at us and make us something new.

I sit at the bar and when he comes up to me, asks me to dance, I move into him, ready to be born. He swims me across the floor, his soft fingers sinking into my flesh and disappearing there. I think, *I am here, now, and nothing is over.* We move like this, like water, the feel of his hands a promise, leaves that will fall, and apples. What matters is not where I have come from, or how long it has taken to arrive, or that Hugh will wake up soon and wonder where his wife has gone. What matters is that she is in my bed right now, filling my house with sleep, dreaming, just waking, waiting for me.

FESTIVAL

There were these things I saw through the window: our parents' coffee table, askew, furrows in the carpet from where it usually sat—that's how well I could see. The light was on, dim light but enough—it was dark where I stood in the backyard, outside the living room window. So, there was the table, the couch of nubby plaid, my sister on her back, head hung over the armrest, blonde hair brushing the floor, and on my sister was a boy whose name I've since forgotten, jeans crumpled to his knees, skinny hips, white ass, rocking himself into her like that.

Then I was fifteen, old enough to know enough to watch—that would be me in a year, I thought, standing in the backyard, waiting for the dog to finish, cold wet grass and weeds scratching at my legs. I moved closer to the window, to the side, my cheek almost against the brick of the house, angling, squinting. Watch, I thought, this is a thing I need to know.

This boy on my sister, on her pretty white skin. We'd slept together, my sister and I, curled into her narrow bed after our mother turned out the light. After she shut the door I left my own bed, fit myself against my sister like a snail to its shell, my face in her tangled hair. She smelled like yewberries then, at eight or nine, still taller than me and thin, dirty feet, hands stained red from berry paint.

I pressed my face against the house, shooed the dog away, watched this boy on top of her. I watched the shadows on the ceiling, shaped, humped, moving in almost even time, sharp above the lamp and blurry farther out. I watched my sister's hands on his back, gripping the cheap fabric of his shirt, and my own hands were clenched, tight against my legs. I was afraid to open them. I watched until I saw the last thing before they finished: beyond the couch, up three steps to the doorway of the kitchen, the wall there covered with pictures of us, straw hats, sunburns, sand, our father lifting us both above a wave, one on either hand—there our father stood.

If my sister had lifted her head, had opened her eyes enough to see, their eyes would have met. I watched our father watching them, my sister in between us with her hair dragging the carpet and her arms twisted above her head in tangled sleeves.

I cannot, now, imagine his face, shadowed, outlined, nothing more. I thought he must have had no face, not then, not watching that—how would that face look? Mouth set or slightly open, eyes bleary or not, hooded, red-rimmed, shot through with gin-soaked veins? His little girl, his darling—I knew who he loved best.

My sister taught me this: that our father could be charmed, teased, bought—with drinks at the door when he got home, with kisses to the back of his neck as he bent over the paper, with perfume behind our ears at dinner. Our mother was no competition for her. Our mother, who had been beautiful, had woken one morning in a house that was no longer hers, had woken to find it given over to her older daughter. Walls, windows, doors, fingerprinted and smudged, strands of my sister's hair like voodoo trails all over.

They slept in separate beds, our parents, the reach of a night table between them, their door open across from our closed one, and in my sister's bed I smelled yewberries, faint, bitter, and early in August. We mashed them in the backyard into paste, striped our cheeks and foreheads, sharpened sticks the length of babies' arms into spears. My arms were mapped with scratches, scabbed and then picked clean. We had the same hands, thin-skinned, backs traced by veins in winter, dark with dirt and sun in summer, too smooth yet to be leathery. Our feet, too, the same, narrow and bony, *toes like monkeys,* said our father, long and grasping. My sister could write her name with a marker held in her curled toes.

✦　　✦　　✦

My sister's husband, the first time we were together, said to me, *She told me the two of you were the same.* He wrapped his hands in my hair, darker than hers and never quite as long, and pulled until my head rocked back, until I thought my breath would stop. He licked the sweat that slicked my throat and ran between my breasts. We were in my bedroom which was hot and oven-close, windows facing an alley, the back lot of a church. There was a festival, the bingo hall, the wheel of fortune, the priests who sat at paper-covered tables and ate sausage wrapped in dripping napkins and foil. There were the smells of grilling meat and fried dough, burnt sugar, sweat and sweet perfume.

My sister's husband told me things about her I already knew. He told me he loved her and he told me how much.

✦   ✦   ✦

Yewberries are poisonous. Our mother scrubbed our hands and faces with soap and disinfectant. She dusted tables and polished mirrors, served us dinner. She never wore an apron. On her dresser were jars and bottles, makeup I never saw her wear. We used this, then, after the berries, warpaint first and then done right, lips red, eyes lined, practicing. We sat for dinner one night like that, and our mother said, *Get that garbage off your faces. I will not have that at my table.*

For our mother, it was that simple—the protocol, the rules, the things we could not do. We knew not to set the table with napkins laid on plates, with goblets upside down.

Later, through the bedroom wall, *Your daughters run wild, Richard, like trash.* And our father's voice, indistinct, not soothing, and the clink of ice on glass. When the lights were out I heard him walking, his tread uneven, one step heavier than the other. He limped, a fracture badly healed, his car accordioned a year before. I knew when he stood in our bedroom doorway: that tread, the creak of door, the smell of cigarettes still on his shirt from work. This was a smell I hated, a smell I pulled away from when I hugged him every night, the smell of where he'd been. I didn't think of this until later, until after my sister had gone and I stood waiting by the side of the road for a car that didn't come, waiting for that boy to come for me like he had come for her, lighting one cigarette off the end of another.

Now, I time myself. A cigarette on the hour, every hour—not even a pack a day. There are lines around my mouth, at the corners of my eyes. Suck, pull, squint. I am aging by the clock.

✦   ✦   ✦

The boy that night was Joe, or Jim, I think—the name on the patch of a shirt I'd seen him wear before, the kind mechanics wear. He got it used for a quarter, from a bin at the back of a thrift store, wrinkled and stained. Our father watched that inside his daughter, a boy in a shirt with someone else's name on it, and I waited outside the window, how long? Only minutes, I think, with the dog whining at my ankles, waiting. Ten years later I stood next to the altar, watching her on our father's arm, coming almost crooked down the aisle, almost lurching our father was by then, and I thought the limp was hers, that by the time they reached the altar I would have to hold her up. Across from me the groom cleared his throat, coughed, looked down at his shoes. Our father's eyes up close were yellowed, and I thought for just one moment that he would stop, refuse to take another step, that he would pick my sister up and run with her, back up the aisle and out the door.

✦ ✦ ✦

Her husband called me on a Sunday, after how many months? Not even a year. He called and said, *Please, meet me, I need to talk to you.*

It would be a lie for me to say I didn't know then. I dressed, nothing special, not outright, and black silk underneath. He would tell me there were problems, he would say they were her fault, and I would believe him because it would be easy, because I would have no reason not to. I put on lipstick and perfume and got into my car, thinking. I would say, *She is difficult, she has always been difficult. You are not to blame if she lies to you, if she hides things from you. We all know.* I would put my hand on his and speak quietly, make him lean to hear me. *Do you want me to talk to her,* I would say.

As it happened, I bought him a drink and listened to him talk about her, things I'd heard before in my mother's voice. *Anything that happens to her will be your fault, Richard, do you understand that?* We sat in a bar for an hour before leaving. He followed me back, parked in the back lot of the church. As I walked up the steps, opened my door, and let him go in first, I thought, This is the worst thing I've ever done, the one unforgivable thing, and there will be no witnesses.

I waited for someone to stop me. I stood in front of him and unbuttoned my shirt, stepped out of my pants, waiting for him to say, *Don't do this.* I stood in that underwear I'd bought with my sister, had let her pick out, and never worn because I didn't wear things like that. I stood, waiting, waiting for anything, for my father's voice in my ears, for his face

I couldn't see from where I stood that night. My sister's husband put his tongue in my mouth and I thought I tasted her.

+   +   +

Once, not long after my sister had gone, I climbed from my window and ran down the street, ready to spread my legs in the back of a stolen car. I walked two miles. I stood at the locked gate of a park by the road, leaned up on the chain link fence, and smoked. I waited an hour before turning back, before walking home thinking, *There was an accident, he got caught, got arrested,* and wanting these things to be true.

When I got home every light in the house was burning. *Stupid little whore,* my father said at the front door, my mother behind him, shaking. He caught me by my hair, pulled me in, his bad leg dragging, catching on the carpet's edge. His glass was on the coffee table, the ice cubes melting, condensation puddling on the wood already shadowed by old water stains. When he slapped me his hand was cold and wet. *I should take your pants down,* he said, *but that's been done already.*

All right, I thought, think that, it's the easy thing, the thing you've gotten used to.

+   +   +

He hadn't stopped them, that I know. I didn't watch them finish. I sat down in the grass, the dog's head in my lap, his wet nose quivering, snapping at nightbugs. I didn't hear them finish, but if I had, would I have known the sound—a choke

48

of breath, a long exhale? I didn't hear our father walk away—
it must have been so hard for him, to be that quiet on his leg,
to balance all his weight on the sloping kitchen floor. There
was no sound that night until the boy's car pulled away, and
even that was not so loud—distant, low in the humid air, giving out to crickets and the whining of the dog.

✦   ✦   ✦

There was, at the festival, a wooden pole, twenty-five feet
high and covered in grease that dripped and ran in the sun.
Men lined up beneath it, shirts off and given to their mothers
or wives to hold. They covered their bare chests with sawdust
from a pile at the base of the pole, slapped it onto arms and
legs, rubbed it between their sweating palms. Each, in his
turn, attempted to climb. There was a cloth affixed to the top
of the pole, and this had to be grabbed.

From my bedroom window I could see them climb: the
tops of their heads, hair matted with sweat and sawdust,
faces tilted back or pressed to the slick wood, eyes squeezed
shut to the glare of sun. The best came close, gripping with
chalked knees, bare feet, and taped hands, sunburnt shoulders bunched and knotted, gaining inches, half a foot, then
slipping, praying for a rough spot where the grease had
melted off. Some bled before they fell, and each was allowed
three tries before moving to the side.

There was a band as well, and majorettes around the pole,
girls eleven and twelve, most of them heavy, their wide dark
nipples showing through the bodysuits, or else in bras that

held up nothing, the flesh of their legs jiggling as they tossed and dropped batons. We had never looked like that, never been so soft and doughy. Our mother would not have had it. She starched and ironed t-shirts, made sure our nails were clean before we went to bed.

Our father took us on his lap until we no longer fit, even with our legs curled tightly to one side, and even then my sister kept on, twisting herself, tucking her knees up under her shirt until it was stretched and torn. In the summer, he held her there on the back porch, both of them watching my mother and me kneeling in the garden, digging rows for lettuce and for mint. If someone had seen us then he would have smiled, thinking only of how lucky our parents were with their two girls, their garden, and their house.

My mother taught me to pile dead leaves around the lettuce to protect the soil from the scorch of sun. She worked with heavy gloves on, her fingers moving through the earth and leaves, faster than I could barehanded. With me, though, she was patient; she had learned that much.

If someone had been watching he would have imagined our table at night: tomatoes and cucumbers piled, fresh mint and basil, the kitchen door opened onto our backyard, and peach soufflé for afterward, because our mother's hands could do that, could coax up eggs and milk and fruit, suspended, quivering.

Her silence I perceived only in relief, I recognized only when I heard her voice at night, rising up through the vents in our bedroom floor, or coming shrill from across the hall.

I thought, *What has my mother said today, what has she said before now?* I heard my sister's name, enunciated, drawn out, my mother's voice insistent over her husband's slurring. My mother had been to college.

What are you teaching her? I heard my mother say, as clearly as though she were in bed next to me. *Do you have any idea what will happen to her after you're done with her? I won't let you do this with the other one, Richard. Not with her, not both of them, not both my girls.*

I had never heard her call us *mine.*

My face was to my sister's back, scratched by brambles from the woods behind our house, drops of drying blood on her nightgown, bits of bark still in her hair our father's brush had missed. When he came up to our room he knelt beside the bed and laid his head on the flowered sheet. I didn't move or turn; I could hear my mother moving in their room, the clink of jars on the dresser, the creak of closet doors, and our father's catch of breath in a haze of gin and lime. My sister slept on, turned away from me beside our father's hands.

✦   ✦   ✦

There is no one thing that I remember, not before I watched that boy on top of her, nothing even after. She circled my father like some small moon, kept at no great distance by any force of gravity on either side of that night—before, after, there was no difference I could see. When she packed to leave, my mother and I sat at the kitchen table, waiting. The kitchen door was open, the grass outside high, brown-tipped towards the field behind our lawn where my father never watered. There were forsythia and pussy willow edging the garden, a vase of them on the table. The dog lay between our feet. We drank iced tea with mint.

+ ✦ +

I thought, If someone gets to the top of the pole and manages to snatch the cloth from it, one quick turn before sliding down and he would see us, would see my sister's husband pulling me to him by my ankles across the bed.

After my father slapped me my mother followed me to my room, closed the door behind us, and took me in her arms. I wore no makeup, I had no money, my hips were still narrow like my father's. The window I'd climbed from was open. She turned down my sheets and took my clothes as I stripped. She brought her pillow in from her bed, propped it against the wall, and sat.

The next morning she had not moved, not that I could see. My clothes were folded on my sister's bed.

The festival ends today. The crowd is denser, men pressed around the stalls. My sister's husband leans from my window, naked, visible to the line of his hip for anyone who wants to know. His back is slick, his hairline almost dripping. I think he could climb the pole; if he were my husband I would want him to.

He has told me, these past days, that he does not know what to do. He says this over endlessly, as though by saying it he will somehow come to understand. *I can't make her hear me,* he says.

I have no explanation. I think of her, of sleeping at her back, of the paint striped on her skin. I tell him, *I don't know her.* I say, *I only know the things I saw. She has her secrets.*

But this is not enough. I could say to him, Did she tell you what our father saw? Did she tell you what she let him see? I could say, If it had been me, he would've beaten me until I couldn't move, torn my hair out by the roots. I have no doubts, none.

We are not the same, I tell him.

In my garden, I would plant tomatoes and cucumbers, I think. Peppers and lettuce, dark green and leafy. There is no room for that here, for mosquitoes and caterpillars, forsythia. But I would fill it with parsley, mint, small shoes, plastic shovels, dolls, tiny arms and legs on climbing vines, sun-warmed and fleshy.

Outside my window I can see the procession: the pastor of the church in gold and crimson robes and behind him the other priests, the extraordinary ministers and their wives. The last, finally, are the nuns, habits billowing in the hot wind, rosaries twisted through their fingers. They walk behind the float, a statue of the Virgin Mary crowned with plastic dimestore flowers on a wheeled plywood frame. They walk and parents push their children forward with money clenched in greasy fingers, bills the nuns attach to money clips that line the edges of the float, and their faces shine with rapture.

SPICE

I have been married for three years now, and my parents and husband get along, in their way. My parents don't come often to our house: we live outside the city, a little over an hour's drive, and my father's sight is failing. But we go there, my husband and I, every other week on Sunday, and I bring things to my mother—brown leather gloves to wear to church, a pair of small earrings. On these Sundays, my husband and father sit together by the television and my mother sets up card tables for them with bowls of olives and peppers and fried smelts draining on paper towels. My husband had never eaten like this. We had to explain the smelts to him—small fish, deep-fried and eaten whole, with heads and bones and tails.

Like peanuts, my father said to him, laughing, *you eat them like peanuts.*

My father has become a man who laughs often, and my mother beside me in the kitchen says, *I just don't know. I worry, I don't know what he thinks is so funny.* But for my part, I suspect that my father laughs not because anything is funny but simply because he is suddenly able to, because there is time for him now. He jokes with my husband and kisses me often when we are there. My mother tells me that he wants to take her dancing on Friday nights at the lodge in the neighborhood. This too is a cause for alarm to her—she imagines that he is becoming frivolous, that he doesn't recognize the fact that he has become old, that he fails to treat their ages with the proper gravity.

On these Sundays, my mother will sit across the kitchen table from me as though I have never left, fingering the gloves or the earrings I've brought her. She will tell me about the people in the neighborhood.

Marie's pregnancy is not going well. The doctors suspect toxemia.

Jimmy's father has had another stroke and will not be leaving the hospital anytime soon, if at all. Jimmy and his wife are taking care of the mother.

Delano's store was robbed again, the third time in as many months. The neighborhood is going down, she says. *The neighborhood is going down.*

From the next room, I can hear my husband and father shouting at a ball game on the television, and when it is over, my husband and I will say our good-byes and get into our car and drive from the parking lot out of the city, and I will tell him most of what there is to tell.

✦　　✦　　✦

It had been a spice factory, where that lot is now, five stories of faded brick, the first floor converted to a gift shop and museum, glass cases filled with doilies, trivets, dried flower arrangements and wooden racks, all manner of things quilted and embroidered.

They began tearing it down in June, slowly, piecemeal, using cranes, hoses, wrecking balls. It could not be imploded because of the new glass-fronted hotel across the street, the danger of the glass cracking, shattering, raining down on the heads of tourist families and businessmen on convention.

There were three separate shifts of workmen who came that summer: the first starting at six A.M., the second relieving the first at noon. The ones who came in the evening were the lucky ones, working short hours from six to eleven in the coolest part of the day and on into the night. Although it was always humid the slight drop in temperature made the closeness more bearable, and the men who worked this shift were loud, joking, shouting things to the people who stopped to watch and teasing the neighborhood boys who rattled the temporary chain-link fence and tossed small stones at one another.

These boys came mostly from two streets over, away from the harbor and the new hotel and the small glittering shops that surrounded it. This street, like the ones that ran perpendicular to it, was narrow and dark and lined on both sides by row houses that seemed in their age to lean in towards one another, as if the weight of the generations who lived in them was becoming heavier with each passing season, floors sagging and marble stoops cracking with the weight of women

Eddie, since then, had gotten the stitches out, but the scar remained. After the other boys tired of looking at it, of touching the shiny white of it with dirty fingers or asking him to fold his lower lip down so they could see the inside, Eddie had taken to sitting on the stoop close against his father, a big man with faded tattoos on his arms and a gold crucifix on a heavy chain around his neck. *Why don't you go play,* his father would prod him, *or at least run to the store and get me a pack of cigarettes,* but Eddie refused repeatedly until his father became frustrated and, cursing, got up to get the cigarettes himself, leaving the boy alone on the stoop. After a few minutes of sitting, chin cupped in his hands, he would get up and move back into the darkness of the house, hovering shadowy in the doorway for a moment before disappearing entirely.

This was the way these streets moved in the summer at night, passing cars infrequent enough for the children to play kickball without interruption for three or more innings, illuminated by streetlights and the higher brighter glow of the floodlights trained on the spice factory two streets over. That was where the traffic was, too, concentrated by the waterfront on the main north-south thoroughfare of the city, and this was where the older boys from the neighborhood sometimes took their girls. These could not be called dates, precisely—the boys' idea of *dates* came from the television. It involved picking up a girl in a car and meeting her parents, shaking the hand of her father and promising to have her home at a decent hour. They had no cars, for the most part, or none that ran reliably, and their parents had all grown up together, gone to the same school and church, so that the notion of actually *meeting* anyone filled them with a quick hot dread—this was not a thing they had to do, or knew how to do, beyond grunting an acknowledgment to a customer's *thank you* as they handed her the groceries they had just bagged.

And there was this: these boys knew enough that *dates* involved the expenditure of money, usually more than the price of a soda or a pack of cigarettes—in short, more than they could afford. And so they waited in loose knots on the street for the girls to come out to their stoops—showered and powdered after dinner, their hair carefully teased and sprayed, smelling of drugstore perfume and strawberry-flavored lip gloss. Boys stood, nervously talking and feinting punches until the girl each waited for appeared, then walked off towards her parents' or grandparents' house to exchange a few words before suggesting a walk to the water.

They waited to take the girl's hand until they had turned the corner at the bus stop. They offered, standing at the crosswalk, to light a cigarette for her, cupping their hands against the wind blowing from the harbor, and discreetly wiped any saliva from the filter before handing it to her. They were not without manners, these boys, no matter that most were tattooed before graduating high school, if indeed they did graduate, jailhouse-tattooed with a needle and India ink, girls' initials on slender biceps or wrists. These manners they did not learn from the television, but from watching their fathers' clumsy dance of chivalry with their mothers or grandmothers—the holding of doors or of coats for the women to shrug into.

So they would walk with the girls to the harbor, crossing between the factory and the hotel in light that was brighter than any on their own streets in the falling dusk. They walked on the bench-lined brick promenade, through families in white shorts and sandals, the children carrying ice-cream cones that dripped and ran down their arms, chins smeared with chocolate, usually, or sometimes strawberry. You could not see their neighborhood, the row houses or marble stoops, the chairs on the sidewalks. What you could see were the lights of the ships in the harbor, the glass elevators that moved up and down in the front of the hotel, and the wrecking ball, knocking chunks of brick and mortar to the upper floors of the spice factory, tearing holes in the exterior of the building that grew in uneven circumference, window frames long emptied of glass disappearing as their boundaries were de-stroyed.

They walked the length of the promenade, talking occa-sionally or not at all, the boys acknowledging someone they knew with a nod then waiting, smoking, side by side, as the girls moved off a few paces from them and leaned in to whis-per and giggle. They had no idea what the girls talked about at these moments and would not have thought, afterwards, to ask—they imagined that this was not a thing for them to know, the secret words of the women who slept next to them, the language they spoke with one another.

The girls, almost without exception, were beautiful. Their skin was smooth and fine, more delicate than one would think they had a right to, unblemished by layers of makeup or the cheap cold cream of their grandmothers, their hair worn long and painstakingly curled. Sometimes, when a girl walked on these nights that could not be called dates, one of the men in white shorts would turn quickly and glance back at her as she walked away from him, at her legs in too-tight jeans and short high-heeled boots. The boys knew this and were proud, although they would not have admitted to it.

After walking the length of the promenade, stopping for a large soda to share, the boys would take the girls to the hill at the far end of the harbor—it was steep, grassy, and out of reach of the streetlights, dotted here and there with the blankets of picnickers. They climbed to the top and sat, without a blanket, sometimes spreading out the boy's flannel shirt if the grass was particularly damp. From the top they could see the line of buildings that separated their neighborhood from the brighter lights of the waterfront, from the traffic and crowds, and they felt lucky for that, protected. The girls felt secure in the thought that they would not have to worry about whom to marry, or when—they would marry the boy who got them pregnant, and as quickly as possible. This was not necessarily a cause for shame to them, though they would not have admitted to thinking it consciously or planning it or even allowing it to happen out of thoughtlessness or lust—it was simply a thing that their friends and sisters had done, and often their mothers before them.

The boys, for their part, would not have to worry about commuting to work through heavy traffic from a house outside the city or having their suits cleaned in time for a business trip—they would dress in the heavy pants and boots of their fathers and grandfathers and take the bus, one transfer, to the steel mill. The boys were at ease with these thoughts and only when they looked at the clouds of dust rising from the wrecking ball at the spice factory did they feel a quick cold stab in their guts, and when this happened they would turn, hands on the girls' waists under the thin fabric of their blouses, and rock back against the slope of the hill, pressing their warm narrow chests on top of them.

Although I am married now, my initials have not changed: there is a boy in that world who could still claim me.

✦   ✦   ✦

I tell my husband about the houses and the smells of the houses; the way the hardwood floors, once polished, were pocked and giving in spots, rotted through sometimes to the planking beneath, or the concrete basements that were damp with mildew through most of the year. Some of these houses have finally, in the past five or ten years, been sold from their families to young couples from out of town, transferred by work. Before moving in these couples pay to have the houses gutted and renovated, to have blond-wood chopping islands put into the kitchens, to have the cheap paneling torn from the front-room walls.

When my mother says that the neighborhood is going down I wonder which part of it she means. I look, sometimes, walking from our car to my parents' front door, at the houses that have been renovated, imagining that people like me must live there now. And I look too at the other houses, the ones I remember, unchanged, and I know that people like me live in those as well.

S P I C E

The spring before the spice factory was torn down, a girl named Gina Capello tried to kill herself. We had not been close, but I knew most of the details, heard in bathrooms and cafeteria lines. There was no one to tell me directly, and it would be a lie for me to say now that I was bothered by this. Because I was not included in the way I had been once, I was saved from having to express shock and sympathy and disapproval and hopes for her speedy recovery and wonder at whether she would graduate with the rest of us in the course of one conversation. I was saved from being expected to stop by her house after school and pretend that nothing had changed, that no one knew or cared, to say, *You should have seen Margaret's hair today,* or *You'll never guess who was kissing on the back of the bus.*

Gina, upon confirming that she was pregnant, had locked herself in her bathroom and cut her wrists with a blade pried from a disposable razor. This was a thing that happened on television shows, not in our neighborhood, and the source of the whispering at school and the clucking of parental tongues was the fact that she had attempted something so melodramatic, so out of proportion to the problem, so *unnecessary.*

As it happened, Gina Capello graduated but did not cross the stage with the rest of us. Her wrists were stitched and bandaged and the blouses she wore for the rest of that warm spring were long-sleeved, buttoned tightly. Shortly after the graduation exercises she and the boy were married in a small ceremony at the neighborhood church. I went with my parents and sat between them in the back row, wearing a black dress I had not worn since my birthday. My mother, I remember, did not speak to me any more than she had to that day, partly because she believed that black was an inappropriate color to wear to a wedding, but mostly, I think, because we had not been included in any of the preparations for the wedding or invited to the reception, a slight that she imagined to be my fault.

That August, my mother ran into Mrs. Capello at the grocery store, who volunteered that Gina and her husband were doing quite well, living with his family, and that she and some of Gina's friends had planned a baby shower for that weekend. Out of politeness, Mrs. Capello asked about me, said that no one had seen me around much that summer, and my mother told her that I had been busy packing for college, choosing my classes, and filling out registration and financial aid forms. When my mother told me about this conversation, I imagined Gina in her family's living room, surrounded by pink and blue streamers and balloons and the girls we had grown up with, wearing a frilly maternity dress that perhaps did not have long sleeves, tearing open wrapped and ribboned boxes. I thought of Gina and her husband who had sat next to me in an advanced math class we had both taken, and I thought of the boy whose name my mother had never mentioned since the night of my birthday.

✦   ✦   ✦

This boy who could still claim me—he has the shadow of my initials still on his arm—instead of a needle and ink used a knife to carve them in, then tapped embers from his cigarette into the cuts, grinding them deep with his thumb. It was my birthday and I was wearing a black dress, the first black dress I had ever owned. I had seen it on the sale rack in an expensive store and dragged my mother there, tried it on again, and spun around in front of her and the three-way angled mirror and the saleswoman. It was beautiful, sleeveless, long and narrow and plain, the kind of dress I had never seen any of the girls in the neighborhood wear: they would have said, *there's nothing to it, what's the big deal?*

So I wore it, the night of my birthday, with my hair slicked back smooth and small silver earrings, and the boy I was with said to me, *Wait in the other room for a minute, I have a surprise for you.* So I got up and left the room and waited, expecting a necklace or charm bracelet. When he called me back he was sitting where I had left him, his sleeves rolled up, holding out one of his forearms for me to see, blood smeared on the skin there and dotting the front of his shirt and his mother's couch, the cigarette still burning in the ashtray and his pocketknife laid across it. He held out his arm for me and picked up the cigarette with his other hand and dragged from it. *Happy birthday, baby,* he said to me, *I love you.*

I have wondered often, since then, what would have happened to me if I had stayed, if I had not simply picked up my coat and purse and left that boy sitting in his mother's basement with blood on his clothes and the smell of his own burned flesh in his nostrils. I have wondered, too, what he told the girl he married not long after that, or what he tells her now when she cries next to him at night, the sound of her own sobs drowning out those of the baby's in the next room, how he explains those marks to her. Scars fade, that I know, but the cuts on his arm were deep.

On that night I left and walked the short blocks to my parents' house, walked past my mother waiting up for me in the living room without a word. In my own room I stripped and hung the dress on a padded hanger, the only one I had. I pulled a plastic garment bag over it and hung it in the back of my closet.

✦   ✦   ✦

After that Monday, things were easy for me. I remember walking into the school, not even worrying that I would see the boy at lunch, because the problem was more immediate than that. No one cleared a path for me in the halls, and no one whispered, at least not that I could hear, because none of that was necessary. The talking had been done, over the Saturday and Sunday, and there was nothing left to say: the conversation was over, the outcome decided. I spoke to no one, and when I got home that afternoon there was a note on the table for me from my mother. She wanted to talk when she got home from work; she came home early and asked me what I had done.

She said she had heard things. She said she was afraid they were true.

The boy's mother had called her, *Your girl,* she'd said. *I'm afraid of what happened. He won't talk to me, won't tell me or his father nothing. But something happened to my boy.*

And my mother had been caught, ashamed, because she

knew nothing, because whatever had happened I was keeping from her, though neither she nor I mentioned the boy's name. She sat patiently at the kitchen table and waited for me to say what I had to say. I still wore my school uniform, white blouse and plaid skirt, the hem held up in spots with staples and Scotch tape.

Mrs. Marinelli called me, she said. *She doesn't know what happened between you two but he wouldn't go to school today. And it doesn't look good, me not knowing what to say to her.*

And I thought, then, that I had not, in fact, seen him at lunch, but I had not really seen anyone at lunch—I had walked into the cafeteria with my head down, found a corner table, and propped a notebook in front of me, reading over and over a page of history notes until the words lost all meaning, until the letters resembled hieroglyphs, strange lines and curves running in random sequence across the paper, ink dotted and slashed in no pattern that I could recognize. He could have been standing two feet in front of me and I would not have seen him. I would have refused to see him, his dark hair and eyes, his pretty shoulders that I had rested my head on in the back seats of cars and the basements of our friends' houses, his shoulders that I had scratched and bitten as I sat naked on his lap, my legs around his waist, feet locked at the small of his back as he moved beneath me.

The thing that my mother was afraid to hear was not that I had slept with him, but that I had left him, because for me to leave him so easily, so quickly, without thought or fear as I had done, meant that I would leave all of them eventually in just the same way.

I do not remember exactly how long the two of us sat in the kitchen that day. I know that it was a cold day in February and that the thin afternoon sun made the kitchen bright as it set, filling the window and burning through the chain-link fence of our back yard, glaring off the patches of snow still left in the shady end closer to the house.

Please, my mother said, *we can't make it better unless you tell me.*

In that place, there was no clear division of generational loyalties—we were all on our way to where our parents were and so it was pointless to speak badly of them, to exclude or mock them. They knew about our lives because it had not been so long before for them and because we told them.

What did you do? she said to me that day at the kitchen table. *What did you do that you can't tell me?*

+　　+　　+

The city had planned for another luxury hotel to be built after the spice factory was torn down. Fifteen years later there is still no hotel; bookings have, in fact, decreased dramatically in the one already standing—*the neighborhood is going down.* In place of the factory is a corner parking lot with a bullet-proof glassed-in attendant's box. Early bird special, in by eight-thirty, out by four-thirty, six dollars. The boys in the neighborhood work there now.

It was a small thing he did, really, perhaps not something that deserved such an extreme reaction on my part. He had, after all, taken me out and told me he loved me, and I had let him fuck me for that—we had both done everything we were supposed to do according to what we knew at the time. I still cannot say that I walked out of his house that night because of any realization or premonition of what would happen to me if I stayed, if I had let him kiss me and wrap his arms around me while his blood dripped on his mother's couch.

He was married shortly after I left for college. My mother sent me the announcement clipped from the paper, a photograph of a girl I did not know. She had highlighted the name of the groom in the accompanying text. The couple planned to honeymoon in Florida and reside in town.

Now, I think of him rarely, and when I do, I find that my thoughts turn more easily to his wife than to him, to a woman my own age whom I do not know, but who may well know my name, might have learned it from someone in the neighborhood or from her husband, who might have asked him once or many times about the shadows of cuts on his arm until he told her as much of the story as he could.

Or perhaps not. He could have that secret. It is one I keep from my husband—in all the times we have talked about the people we were involved with before each other I have never spoken of that. It is a story I would not know how to tell him—it is not that my husband is a passionless man, but it makes me uncomfortable to think that he would laugh, or that I would cry if I told him.

The story I do not know how to tell my mother is that we have been trying to have a baby for the past two years, and while my husband is patient and kind, I cannot help but think that this is the price exacted from me for the ease of my leaving. I imagine, some months, that what I need to do is tell my husband what that boy did for me, and if my husband thinks it stupid, I would explain to him that it was not. He would not laugh and I would not cry and when we made love afterward I would conceive.

I imagine telling him this. But what I tell him instead is that the summer they tore the spice factory down the dust rose up over our heads and it smelled of cinnamon and nutmeg, that the whole city by the water smelled that summer of our mothers' kitchens, sweet and hot, and when the building was gone we lifted piles of rubble to our faces and it smelled as if the factory were still there.

FULL

They eat. They eat like animals, like pigs at a trough. It is their secret, so secret to each of them that they pretend not to notice it in the other, this way of eating. They stare at the tables, the walls, the food. They are careful in this. They do not dirty plates; they eat from pans, jars, cartons. They use plastic utensils. The silverware gleams dark in its drawer.

They are invited to dinner at her mother's house on weekends and they are strained, ill at ease. The table with its place settings, its crystal and vase of flowers, is foreign to them, strange territory, hostile. They are careful with the cloth napkins, the fragile wine glasses. Her mother is struck by their manners, their reticence. They negotiate the serving bowls and the water pitcher and her mother comments on how quiet they are, how pale her daughter seems. She asks if they eat enough at home. She asks if they would take leftovers. She serves coffee with heavy cream.

Home again, he undresses while she puts the foil-wrapped packages in the refrigerator. He sits in bed with a magazine, a crossword, and she says she is going to get some air. They have a balcony that faces the ocean. She leans on the railing until she sees the light in the bedroom go off, and when it does, she goes inside. She closes the sliding glass door behind her and moves through the dark apartment into the kitchen. She stands barefoot in the light from the open refrigerator. Barefoot, unblinking in the chill, she squeezes anchovy paste from the tube into her mouth.

✦　✦　✦

They have been together for months now, Drew and Alice, living in this apartment on the beach since the beginning of summer. They have their secrets. Not secrets kept deliberately—deliberation implies a choice, and for Alice there is no choice. There is not, for instance, a choice in the matter of her eating. She cannot rightly say that she eats when she is hungry—she has lost all sensation of hunger; she is fast losing her sense of taste. She eats for the texture, for the greasy, gritty feel of potato chips on her fingers, for the sharp crumbs at the corners of her mouth. She dips crab in melted butter until her lips and chin are slick with it. She chews on raw spaghetti, grinding it into tiny sticks. She puts caramels in her cheeks like snuff; with her tongue she rubs them smooth into slippery molds of her teeth. She is never hungry, she is always hungry. She bites into ice cream with her front teeth.

Because Drew does not comment on the taste of what they eat anymore, Alice can only believe that he eats for the same reason she does, for the feel of the food separating between his teeth, for the smooth coating of it on his tongue and the roof of his mouth. Alice examines her own tongue in the mirror, sometimes, expecting that the taste buds will be gone, worn smooth by the constant friction of sucking and chewing and swallowing. She does not tell him this, does not tell him that she can barely remember the difference between sweet and salty.

Neither does Alice tell him that she sometimes pretends they are married, or else that they are children playing house, brother and sister even, tucked into the same bed at night. She pretends this way only when she is alone in the apartment: she finds that Drew's physical presence is an intrusion to these fantasies. He is too real, too solid—and it is because of this that she does not fantasize when they make love. She makes love to him in the way that she eats, with no real awareness of who he is or what he does. She rubs her cheek with the rasp of his beard, with the less abrasive curl of the hair on his chest, with the smooth skin of his belly. She catalogues these things, these moves from texture to texture. She concentrates on the feel of his fingers on her shoulders or hips, the pressure of his hands, the calluses on his palms. If they have been at the beach, the sheets of the bed are gritty with sand, and the grains of it on her sweaty hands make her think of potato chips, of their grease and salt. After Drew has fallen asleep she goes to the balcony and stands, and at night the scent of the ocean seems weaker, less overwhelming. She can easily discern the smell of the pines across the bay on the mainland.

✦　✦　✦

Alice works in a jewelry store; Drew works days on the beach, renting umbrellas and chairs to the tourists, and sometimes rafts for their children. He takes their money and jokes with them, tells the mothers which restaurants on the strip are good with small children, which ones have high chairs and plastic bibs. He tells them that the jewelry store where Alice works is a fine one, reasonably priced, even cheap, which is not true. Alice knows when a customer has been sent by Drew: there is a raised eyebrow, there is haggling over the prices, the quality of a turquoise ring or a locket with hinges that stick.

On the beach at night, behind the blue boxes where the chairs and umbrellas are stored till morning, she tells Drew not to do this, not to send these people to the store. He laughs and says he won't anymore, he promises, really this time, and he kneels in front of her, patting the cool night sand in mounds around her feet. There is wine—there is always wine with Drew, and he holds the bottle to her mouth, tipping it up and farther up until rivulets run down her chin, and the neck of the bottle is gritty with sand. Alice can feel it crunch between her teeth.

These nights Alice pretends that they are young—fourteen, fifteen, the same age as the other couples who huddle on the beach at night. Drew's presence does not hinder this: there is the sound of the waves, the scent of the pines, and the damp dark feel of the sand beneath her bare feet and hands. These are things that surround her, her and Drew both.

These things seem to swallow them up until she can believe that Drew is simply a shadow that can be held and heard, and only that.

She is not good at these games, she knows. If Drew is caught in the spotlight of the beach patrol, if she sees the stubble of his beard, light against his dark skin, or the ragged fingernails of his hand on her leg, she feels suddenly shocked, cheated by the heaviness of him, by the meaty warmth of his flesh, and she can no longer imagine him any other way.

One night, there is a girl standing a few yards away from them, her shoes in her hand, squinting into the darkness, looking for someone.

A boy, probably, Drew says, propping the wine bottle between Alice's legs.

Hey, he yells, you looking for someone? It's awful dark out here.

The girl turns in the direction of his voice, takes a few steps towards them, squints into the darkness.

That could be me, Alice thinks.

The girl says, I'm supposed to meet—

And then another shape appears from the narrow boardwalk that runs from the access road to the beach, a boy-shape, and he grabs the girl around the waist. There you are, she says, laughing. You're late.

They walk off, leaning forward into the small dunes, and Drew reaches into Alice's lap for the bottle, his eyes shut tight, groping at her legs.

There you are, he says, and opens his eyes, grinning, takes the bottle and climbs on her, pinning her against the blue box.

Alice closes her own eyes then, closes them to the hungry cave of his mouth, and drinks the last from the bottle he holds to her lips. She puts her hands up under his shirt, feeling the dark fur of his chest, and the sand.

✦   ✦   ✦

Alice decides that she will make a curry, a spicy one with potatoes and onions and chickpeas. She goes to the store after work and buys these things, plus yellow rice to have on the side. The curry will be spicy, exotic—she has bought the package labeled "hot" and intends to add more chili powder and crushed pepper to it. She thinks there is no way Drew will be able to avoid commenting on it, and perhaps even she herself will be able to taste it.

After she has got the pans simmering on the stove, she takes a drink to the balcony and sits down. The shadows on the beach are long, but there are still families sitting in low chairs under umbrellas that dot the sand. She can see the top of Drew's head from where she sits. He is stacking rafts along the side of the blue box. She remembers being a child and coming in from the beach at this time, her skin tight and salty, and her mother telling her to get the sand off her feet before she came in, and hurry up about it, too, because dinner was almost ready. The taste of those dinners is clear to her even now, somehow, the slight fishiness of everything, the salty dampness, the dishes that were never quite hot enough.

Drew is putting the rafts away. There is only one family, one umbrella, left on his section of the beach, and they are shaking out their towels and blankets, stepping into shorts.

FULL

Alice knows, without even waiting to watch, that once Drew
has closed and locked his box he will take off his shirt and run
down to the water, swim out beyond the breaking of the
waves and back in again, once, towel off, and walk down the
access road to their apartment. He will not stop at the showers to rinse the sand from his feet. He will not bring her shells
or glassy pebbles to put in a ceramic bowl on the table.

She goes inside and adjusts the burners on the stove and
puts down full place settings on the table. There are even
chilled mugs for the beer. There is everything—when Drew
comes in, she thinks, he will sit down and she will serve him
and he will kiss her and exclaim over the food. They will be
just like any other couple in an apartment on the beach, on
vacation or not, because there are still some people who live
here year round despite the miserable economy of the winter
months, and they will eat and drink and talk about their days
at work and their plans for the evening or the weekend. Except that Drew works on the weekends: there is more money
to be made on the beach during the weekends and so he works
longer hours and comes home more tired. And Alice does not
go to the beach anymore during the day. The hours she spent
in the sun growing up here have taken their toll on her skin,
on her face and neck especially. Her fine skin has been creased
and lined and she is not yet thirty. She would never come to a
place like this on a vacation. The ocean is full of jellyfish and
horseshoe crabs, the beach full of sand fleas. Drew's skin is
covered with their bites.

✦   ✦   ✦

Is it good? she says. The food steams in heavy stoneware bowls. The doors to the balcony are open to let in the breeze. The mugs of beer are sweating, puddling on the table. Drew eats steadily, huge forkfuls of rice and curry, his face bent close to the plate.

Do you like it? she says. Do you want more? Can I get you another beer?

He shakes his head, he says he is fine, everything is fine. When he finishes the food on his plate he pushes it aside and rests his elbows on the table. He holds his fork loosely, dips it first into the bowl of rice and then into the bowl of curry. He continues to eat.

Give me your plate, Alice says. She reaches for the serving spoon. Let me have your plate, I'll give you more, there's plenty.

Don't worry about it, he says. This is fine. It's fine like this. It's better like this, he says.

When Alice was a child, she ate ice cream out of the carton. Put it in a bowl, her mother said. Why can't you put it in a bowl? You can always get more.

Because it tastes better this way, Alice would say.

She finishes what's on her plate, pushes it aside, and leans into the bowls at the center of the table. She uses the serving spoon, loading it full and taking mouthfuls off of it. She is aware of the sweat at her hairline and around her mouth. She knows the food is hot. She remembers standing at the stove, shaking in chili powder, chopping shriveled red peppers. At the stove, she wiped her eye without first rinsing her hand and it burned.

When they finish, Drew takes the last bottle of wine from the cupboard, uncorks it, and stands by the door.

This is it, he says, pushing the cork back into the neck, waving the bottle. Remind me to buy more tomorrow.

They walk to the beach, barefoot, holding hands loosely, and settle against the small dune behind the blue box. The beach is crowded tonight. At the next box down, just within earshot, there is a party going on, with beer in coolers and a radio. Drew drinks happily and passes the bottle to Alice.

They're not old enough to drink, he says, gesturing down the beach. Not one of them. He laughs.

Did you do that? he says, squeezing her breast, kneading it until she feels the flesh squeezing through his fingers. She will be bruised in the morning. When you were younger, I mean.

No, Alice says, I never did that. I was shy. I wasn't good with boys.

But of course she did do it, drank on the beach at night and hoped her mother wouldn't see her, because they lived in a small house right on the beach then, before her father became unable to work and moved them to an apartment farther inland. She was exotic to the boys who came with their families on vacations, an unlikely and respected discovery: a *local* girl, one who really did live here year round, who was never pale or flabby, one who could fish and water-ski and bodysurf. They fought over her sometimes, tried to impress her with surfboards or the inflatable rafts that Drew now rents. She never rented anything from the blue boxes. She had her own chair, her own raft. She never sat under an umbrella. The boys' vacations lasted for a week, two at the most, and so there was an endless string, faces pale and then sunburned or else easily tanned, an exchange of phone numbers and addresses, of promises to keep in touch. Sometimes they did, for a few months or sometimes until the next trip to the beach was being planned by their parents. Alice imagined them going home and telling their friends, Yeah, I met someone, and she's a *local*. She *lives* there year round.

There were a few that she saw from summer to summer. There were others whose faces she thought she recognized, but they did not speak, and so she was never sure.

From September to May she sat at a desk in the one high school on the peninsula. Most of the other students were the children of farmers or fishermen. There were electives offered in soil cultivation.

Her father taught at the college, sixty miles away, until he was too sick to work. She did not take the electives. She did not go on dates. She waited for the hotels and apartments to be rented out for the summer. She waited until May.

Drew's hand is still on her breast, but he fingers it lightly, absently. He is still watching the party farther down the beach.

I never did that, she says again.

She watches the party also and squints to make out the faces. She thinks she sees the boy and girl from the other night, but of course it is too dark to be sure.

Look at them, Drew says, awed. I wish I could've done that. I wish I could do that now. *Look* at them.

Alice looks, she watches, and the hand on her breast is heavy again, the fingers squeeze and twist. She watches and thinks of the girls, of what the boys call the girls: *tomato,* and *peach,* and *hot tamale.* She would laugh at this, perhaps, but her breath is caught, clenched beneath the pain in her chest.

✦   ✦   ✦

In bed that night, Alice thinks of the dishes left in the sink, unwashed. She cannot remember the last time either one of them washed a dish. There are leftovers. She mixed the curry and rice together before putting the bowl in the refrigerator. It will become denser, hotter from the peppers in it, the longer it sits.

It sits, it becomes denser and hotter, heavier somehow, and while it sits Drew and Alice make love. Alice can smell the curry, the pepper and garlic and coriander, in his sweat. He reeks of it, he reeks of food, and she is aware in some small way of the taste of wine on his tongue. She sucks at it, at his tongue, she is greedy for it, she gorges. She imagines what it would be like to have no food, to be hungry, really, to know that if she got up during the night and went to the kitchen there would be nothing there. She imagines the children she went to school with who are farmers and fishermen themselves now. She imagines them staring at barren fields, pulling up empty nets, sitting at bare tables. She wonders how long it would take, how many days or weeks, to starve.

Drew moves on top of her, his hands under her, on her

buttocks, squeezing her, and still she has his tongue in her mouth. She bites it, she scrapes it with her teeth, she wonders how hard she could bite before drawing blood, and she wonders also at the taste of his blood, if it would be salty or sweet, if it would taste of the curry they've eaten. She wonders if she could tell; she has never been so hungry.

IN HOUSES

I have had a new face for three months now, three months since my old one was cut. The doctors said to me in the hospital, amazing, amazing that my teeth were all intact, not broken, not one. Amazing that I had not lost one eye or both, amazing that I had not been touched in any other way. This was their way of saying something else. From my neck down, nothing—not a mark.

My nose was rebuilt, and one cheekbone, the eye on that same side. That eyelid still droops, sleepy; there are still fine and curving scars. But I am lucky, though it took some time for me to believe this.

I was cut in the street outside a bar not far from my own neighborhood. It was not an alley and I was not drunk. The streetlights all were working. I was grabbed from behind and cut and dropped and left—quick, painless until later, and now mostly healed. It is true that I still look at strangers longer than I did before, more closely, but this is not out of fear. I imagine sometimes that I will know him, the man who did this to me, my architect, my artist, and when I recognize him I will stop him. I might retrieve a dropped package for him, lay a hand on his sleeve, and smile at his thanks. He will be polite and I will smile through his work.

I have only looked for him so I can forgive him. When I look at myself in mirrors now I grieve not for what I lost, but for what I am still losing: the scars swallow themselves over days, over hours.

✦ ✦ ✦

My younger brother was the one who sat with me in the hospital. Though our parents had died soon after we moved from their house and so released us from any familial obligation to civility, he came to my room every evening, leaving his new wife home to unwrap their wedding gifts. I remember—though this might be inaccurate, a sterile dream—the weight of his forearms at the foot of my bed, the brush of his hair on my shoulder.

I was two when he was born, and as a child I had adored him, imagined him as my mother's gift to me, a small soft animal with the power of speech, a power that left me shaking and cold. My parents had told me so often of my own difficulties in learning to speak, the glottal stops and wet silences, the specialists and therapists, that I supposed my voice would disappear in the way it had arrived, without my knowledge or awareness, that I would wake one morning mute and panicked. I thought of words as objects, dimensional, unwieldy as rocks, stopping up my throat, ready to choke me, and I whispered hoarsely into my brother's ear as I would a doll.

I fed him, stole crackers and bits of cheese and bribed him with these. *Davey, play with me, come to the schoolyard with me, I'll push you on the swing.* If there were other girls playing there, hopscotch or keep-away, I would pull the chains of the swing up short, twist them until he faced me and lean into his hair—*That one with the ponytail, she eats bugs. I saw her.* He listened to whatever I told him without a word, with no indication of either trust or disbelief. *That one doesn't take baths, that one's mother makes her sleep in the attic with the rats.*

Years later, he brought his friends to the house on weekends. One, a tall blonde boy with a wispy mustache, came knocking on my bedroom door while my brother remained outside, on the lawn beneath my window. Late spring, cut grass, slanting sun and pollen—I opened my door and let him in, listened while he told me how pretty my hair was. I could hear my brother on the grass below me, and my father saying he would light the grill. Close to summer, this boy put his mouth on mine—his lips were dry and sour, the pressure of his teeth surprising.

Let me, he said, and moved his hand into my lap. I could smell charcoal, lighter fluid. A faucet ran beneath us in the kitchen. There would be corn, wrapped in foil on the grill, dinner at the picnic table, my parents' pitcher of martinis, sweating cold.

My brother told me later that he had bet on what this boy could make me do. *Five dollars,* he told me afterward, *you made me five dollars. Would've been more if you hadn't made him stop.*

But my brother was the one who waited by my hospital bed for me to wake, to speak, for the bandages to come off, the damage to breathe.

It's not that bad, my handsome brother said when I was unwrapped. *Edie, it's not bad, not at all. They'll fade.*

And in the mirror he gave me I saw it wasn't bad, it was beautiful, no matter his wide eyes, his fixed smile, his voice that I had not heard for so long (his new wife had told me, *I love his voice*)—my face was a topography, lined in red and shadowed, here a river, here a road, and here something fallow, waiting for what might happen. My face was a new map.

✦   ✦   ✦

I often think of houses. There was the one in which my brother and I were born, new-built when our parents moved in, the last on a dirt road. Others like it sprang up fast enough, shuttered and sided; our road was paved and cleared through to another.

There was the house in which I lived when my mother called to tell me my father had died, and the one in which I lived when my brother called to tell me that our mother had. The first was a row house, red brick and narrow, the second large, creaking, and damp. People die.

I have traveled and come back again. I have left flowers and prayer cards on my parents' graves. I have stood at my brother's wedding with a small bouquet, needless tissue wrapped around the stems in case I cried, wearing a pink dress that I have since given away. On the altar, he kissed his new wife with perfect child's lips. Our parents' funerals, his wedding, three times in ten years—this is how often I had seen my brother until he leaned against my railed bed.

The houses are still standing. There is no reason that I can see for a house to stand when the people who filled it have gone. I have never driven back to any place to look in a window, walk on the grass, touch the back door. This is touching the dead, or the living dead: the house where we were born, where my brother and I spent every day fighting our way to the places we are right now, is a breathing grave, a catacomb. The walls and floors may as well be dirt.

The wide front porch, the kitchen that faced the back garden, our parents' blue bedroom—I would go back to these places only to plant crosses in the floors, to pray over them like that, and no matter what a mirror might tell me, I am still too young for this.

✦   ✦   ✦

I have not been back to the place where I was cut, though I tried, not long after I was sent home from the hospital, but when I walked in I saw the bartenders who'd known me, saw their faces like my brother's when the bandages came off, their stillness. Guilt, pity, shame, or none of these things— that was not for me to know. But I was pleased. *Here I am,* I remember saying, stiff through the stitches, their pull and tug. I took the straw from the drink they placed in front of me, lifted the glass to my mouth. The owner came from around the bar to touch my shoulder—*It's good to see you, Edie,* he said, smiling past me. If we had been in my parents' house I would have thrown the drink in his face. I was looking there for someone else, someone I had never seen.

I wonder if he would know me now, my face, his work, in dim light or bright, or from a certain angle. The shirt I was wearing that night was ruined, stained and torn and thrown away like so much garbage. I have tried to find one just like it, and the truth is not that I am looking for him to forgive him, but to thank him.

✦   ✦   ✦

These are the things I think of when I think of my brother David.

He is six and I am eight and we are sitting in the kitchen with our parents, the back door open to a summer night (it was always summer, it seems to me now; there was never the white sky of winter). School is starting soon. *First grade, Davey,* our mother says, and our father cuts a watermelon at the sink. My brother recites from an old reader of mine, pointing at pictures, pronouncing carefully, *Uncle,* he says, *Rooster.* Crickets, frogs, the smell of mint from the garden. My brother is a stringless puppet and the house we are in is huge, preparing to eat its dead.

We are twelve and fourteen and our parents are at the neighbors'. We have been drinking vodka from the bar in the living room, and when we begin to feel it we pour water carefully from a measuring cup back into the bottle. We close the cabinet and go upstairs to brush our teeth, pushing together

through the narrow doorway of the bathroom when we hear
our parents laughing on the walk below us. (This is the sound
of those years—our parents laughing at something we could
not hear, were not meant to hear.) Then they are quiet, and
the sound of the sprinkler in the yard is everywhere. From
the window we see our parents swaying, kissing, and my
brother whispers in my ear, *Look at that. Look at that whore,
Edie. He'll get it tonight.*

I am wearing a yellow nightgown. My brother is in shorts
and a T-shirt. He spits toothpaste in the toilet and leans in to
me, his breath hot mint—*You want to watch? Want to see what
she does to him?*

Fifteen and seventeen and I am old enough. We are in our
parents' house (when have we ever been anyplace else?) in the
heat of July. My brother's friend is on my bed and I am kneeling on the floor at his feet. My brother stands against the
closed door of my room, watching. This is the way we dance,
my brother and I. When my shirt comes off I turn my back to
the door.

In the room we are silent, not because of our parents—
they are below us, talking over music in the kitchen, and
would hear nothing—but because I cannot bear to hear my
brother's voice. The burn of his eyes on my back is enough,
and the boy on my bed is incidental, faceless, frightened of
both of us, my brother and me. Later I will run out to the
lawn while the rest of them sleep, our parents wrapped together and my brother sprawled on top of his sheets and his
friend choking through nightmares in his narrow bed while I

dig my feet in bare damp earth, crushing herbs, hammering out my own steps, like this and like this and like *this*, and where else have any of us ever been, where else could we go?

✦　　✦　　✦

My brother drove me home from the hospital. He wanted to bring me back to the house where he lived with his new wife but I had refused; her shirt that I wore was enough.

"Are you sure you'll be all right?" he asked me, standing on my steps, waiting while I unlocked the door.

"Fine," I said. My face itched beneath fresh gauze, the itch of healing already. He held a bag of creams and lotions the doctors had given me for the scars. I swung the door open and moved aside for him. "If I need you I can call you."

It was difficult for me to move my lips through the stitches, the swelling. My voice was flat, without inflection, hard consonants spoken through mud. He set the bag in the hallway and looked at the wall behind me.

"Edie, I'd really rather—"

"No," I said, or almost. I could not move my mouth around the long *o* and what came out was a negative hum, a song in relief. We might have been children again, with all these years before us, watching our father spin our mother across the front porch, his hand on her hip, while the summer sky opened with rain. We stood in my hallway.

"What about the dermabrasion, then?" he said. "Will you go back for that?"

"David," I said, and I shrugged. I stilled my jaw. I would have asked him, *Do I look like someone you used to know?*

IN HOUSES

I had already decided: I did not want these marks erased, any more than time would allow. My hands were clenched at my sides, ready to fly to my cheeks, peel the bandages off—in time, I thought, my fingers would read my flesh like Braille.

+   +   +

When I was a child, my mother insisted that I learn to cook. We were never left in the care of a babysitter, not after I was old enough to negotiate the kitchen. When our parents went out, to a neighbor's house for drinks or dancing, our mother left a phone number and said, *You two, you'll take good care of one another for me, won't you? We'll be late coming home.* She held her husband's arm, and I remember the fabric of her dresses: brushed cotton, or linen, and our father's seersucker suits.

I made casseroles, macaroni and tinned meat or fish, cans of peas or corn, squares of cheese overlapping on the top, quilting it. I worked at the table, imagining the flush of our mother's cheeks in the heat, her damp hands rumpling our father's suit. I stood at the sink rinsing spoons, and my brother played outside in the dark, digging in the garden for weeds, for worms, working by touch and the light from the kitchen window. I wore my mother's apron.

Years of this and my cooking improved, became more so-phisticated, though every recipe was still made and served in a single dish—stews or chilled summer soups, elaborate cas-soulets—all of them in my mother's deep bowls. My brother and his friends would eat these things before leaving our house to drive through the town, to drink with the girls they knew, girls their own age or younger, girls who would accept the cheap bourbon they were offered and smile, who would drink from the sticky neck of the bottle, brave, gagging from the first sip, their thin legs tight and shaking.

In bed, later, I could hear first my parents then my brother come home. My parents were giggling, murmuring over the rattle of lids and ladles—I left the covered pot of food on the stove for them. Some time after this, after I heard my father's snores, there was my brother on the steps, much quieter than our parents had been, his soft tread stopping outside my door, and his voice, Edie. *Do you want to see Dan tomorrow? Edie?*

The next evening our father would light the grill and make martinis or margaritas. Our mother would make a salad and homemade ice cream for dessert. The radio in the kitchen would be on and my brother and Dan (Doug? Evan?) and I would stay upstairs until we were called. We stayed in my room, in the sticky heat of it, in the green and yellow light there, the pollen floating in the light. We came down for dinner, my brother and I and his silent friend. My parents, who sat shoulder to shoulder, thigh to thigh, who rested their hands on each other's knees during every meal I ever ate with them, would allow us to split a beer with dinner.

✦   ✦   ✦

There will be the house in which I live when my brother's wife calls to tell me that he has died. I have not yet imagined what this house will be like, any more than I have doubted that my brother will die before me, any more than I have wished for my face back whole again. I have been opened up, rewritten.

In the hospital, the evening nurse was young. If she came into my room while my brother was there she blushed and ducked out quickly, waiting until he left before returning. She told me one night that when she was a child, her mother had left all the doors of their house open—this was in the country. When my nurse had gone home recently to visit, she told me, she had walked through the open front doorway to find two chickens in the hall and another in the kitchen, pecking at the floor around her mother's feet while her mother made iced tea. That one was the favorite, my nurse said. Her mother called him Horace.

No one will have lived before in the house where I will live when my brother dies. It will be quiet there. I will spend my time in the kitchen, at the stove. I will be stirring something when his wife calls to tell me what has happened.

After the funeral, I will bring her back to my house and tell her about my brother when we were children and I was afraid to speak. I will tell her about the playgrounds, the school-yards and sandboxes. I will say that he was always handsome, fragile, and then not. I will tell her how we watched our parents dance, no matter their missteps in the grass or on the uneven linoleum of the kitchen, the spilled drinks and puddling ice cubes, the ice cream cones melting down my mother's wrist. *We loved to watch them,* I will say to her, *David loved that. The way my father spun her.* I will say these things to my brother's widow, and we will both cry in my house. We will grieve.

In the hospital, the doctors picked gravel from my opened cheeks with tweezers.

My brother's widow will leave my house to go back to

hers, a house like any other standing, a house reeking of the dead, and my parents will still be dancing.

I would tell the man who remade me something different. I would tell him how I cooked for my brother, how I fed him—the careful soups: carrots, sweet peppers, chicken, bones for flavor (I always told him, *Be careful of the bones*). I would tell him how I knelt in the garden in the early dark, collecting what I fed him—small onions, parsley for garnish, pebbles, smooth stones, silver-gray, salted and simmered, peppered with earth, coming to rest at the bottom of the pot, scraping there. *(Have you had enough, Davey? Can I get you more?)*

I would ask this man, *When people die do they remember? When they dance do they remember? Does the body remember, the flesh, the skin, the way it used to move and breathe?*

I would say, *Dance with me, it's been so long. Come to my house so I can feed you. There's a chill.*

I would position myself—foot arched, calf tensed, ready—and draw him to me, hips angled and close. *Like this*—

On my count—hand to hand, hand to waist, beneath the new moon of my face, and we would begin.

NICE GIRL

I was a nice girl, I can say now, if memory serves me. But memory is a tricky thing, given to strange twists and occlusions, slippery in its way, or else easily contained, closed off, harnessed and shut down. *I've forgotten,* I could say, about anything I choose, though this may not be true. I could say that I've forgotten about my sister, drowned when I was five, that all I know of her are the dates on the marble tombstone, the inscription *Little One*. Not true, this. I know that she was not so little, older than me by three years and tall for her age, and heavy. I know these things not because I was told, but because I remember. I know that I was there when she drowned, lying by the side of the pool in our backyard, with a coloring book and crayons that were slick and waxy in the sun.

In this memory, my sister is practicing her dives in the shallow end of the pool, obedient even in our mother's brief absence—we were not to swim in the deep end unsupervised.

She dives in and climbs out, dives and climbs, and it is some minutes after I hear the muted thud that I realize, that I look up to see her beneath the sunny rippled water, on my belly on the tile, waiting to see if she will move or float before I call our mother.

A suburban accident, prosaic, a matinee, not worth the time it takes to tell it.

My mother says I screamed.

She says that she heard me from the kitchen doorway where she had gone to answer the phone—this happened long before there were cordless phones in every house like ours. She says my scream was not so loud because I had not moved from where I lay on the edge of the pool, screaming down into the water at my sister for our mother—who became, that day, my mother.

She came running down the long green slope of lawn and hauled my sister out, dragging her backwards up and out of the pool, heels knocking on the concrete steps. She had my sister by the tops of her fleshy arms and knew nothing but to lay her on her side and pound her on the back to get the water out, and then to lift and shake her, head falling forward and back, her wet hair soaking my mother's shirt.

My mother ran back up to the house. She left me to keep watch.

✦   ✦   ✦

Today, I am thin like a runaway, like a viney plant. My mother fed me with pears and crackers, slices of broiled chicken. She sent me off to school with carrot sticks and celery stalks, and there was toast when I got home.

Those afternoons, in our kitchen, she sat with me while I did my homework. She did not offer to help but neither did I ask, preferring instead the near-silence of my pencil on the pulpy lined tablet, the drip of water in the sink. If she saw me make mistakes—and I often did, in math especially—she did not point them out to me. It was only with my father, only when he took me on his lap after dinner that I realized. He would study the paper and say, "There are two mistakes here, baby. Can you find where they are?"

When he did this I could feel my hands and ears go hot—not with fear, certainly: my father spoke to me with patience and a respect that I was not quite sure I deserved. I would stare at the paper, suddenly realizing that I had been careless, distracted, or too quick in my work, and before I could answer him, or flip my pencil eraser-end to the page—*this one, Daddy, I think*—my mother would put her hand on his shoulder and say, "She's done enough for tonight, Charlie. If it's wrong, it's wrong. They'll correct it in school tomorrow."

What I am saying is that for the years after my sister drowned my mother and I lived in some odd lockstep, terrified to let the other out of sight for too long, or turn our backs. We circled one another like sniffing dogs, leashed to the same stake by no great radius, bound up by all the things not said, not *nice,* by what I believed implicitly were the terms of that mute agreement we had established. My older sister, my mother's firstborn, fat, ungainly, brilliant by all accounts, had been loved unreservedly and feared not a little by us both, and we had failed her. We did not speak of blame or comfort. We did not speak, ever, of the fact that each of us knew too much of the other, that each, in her turn, could suddenly and without breath or kind warning say, *It was because of you.*

+   ✦   +

Years of this, you cannot imagine. It was my habit to occupy the corners of spaces, the backs of rooms, to speak rarely if at all. My teachers, I think, mistook my silence for grief and often touched my shoulder as they passed me, though I cannot truthfully say that I was grief-stricken, not then. Rather, I was cautious, and always watchful of dishonesty.

And I watched the girls, the ones who would have had no traffic with my sister had she lived that long. They were dazzling: faces scrubbed and perfect, small noses, shiny lips that would taste of strawberry or bubblegum, depending on the day. They were vicious, mercenary in their loyalties and swift with retribution for real or imagined wrongs. To say that I liked them would be a lie, a too-easy rewriting of what I know to be true. I believed myself an animal in comparison, a small scuttling thing, mute and nearly blinded by their brilliance.

I learned the word *dyke* and knew that I was not one, which is not to say that I didn't wish otherwise. I liked boys, but only sometimes, and only when I was not too close. They were unmanageable in their physicality: skinny legs and pointy elbows always scraped and scabbed, limbs spilling over the edges of chairs, feet in aisles, as though they hadn't yet mastered the far reaches of their bodies, the extremities of their flesh. Their skins could barely contain them.

But the girls were something different.

+ ✦ +

If you were to ask me now what I am afraid of, I would answer no differently than I would have then.

I am afraid of large groups of people.

I am afraid of whispering behind hands.

I am afraid of being found out.

+ ✦ +

My sister, had she lived, would have been torn to pieces. This is a thing I tell myself still, that I told myself then every night before I slept. Thirteen, fourteen, fifteen—I slept in the bed next to hers, kept as an extra and usually empty, her mattress like new, smooth and firm, the spread aligned, the throw pillow centered exactly.

Thirteen on a Sunday with my parents after Mass—stuffed animals in baskets, prayer cards, a box of sugar candy for Valentine's Day—*kiss me, be mine*. My father propped these things against the headstone, the offering of the living, while my mother gripped my thin arm and did not cry. Tears were a luxury, a temptation, like meat on Fridays: the first step on the path to a place she would not go.

Once home, we separated, my father in the living room and me in the bedroom with my schoolbooks while my mother wandered the house, silent in stocking feet. This

lasted until she could wait no longer and came to stand outside my closed door, still for some minutes before knocking.

"Will you come for a walk with me?" she said, waiting,
still, watching for a sign from me that this was where we'd
start, our words like sucking whirlpools to finish us off on a
sunny winter afternoon.

Watchful me, fingerprints inked on pages—"I can't now,"
the *now* my constant mistake, the thing that gave her license
to come back the next Sunday, and the next, to ask me to walk
with her I thought until the day I died.

"You shouldn't work so much," she said. "Why do you
work so much?"

I am afraid, also, of dying. I was afraid of that early, a quick
and restless fear. I imagined I would die in a car wreck,
strapped in and burnt or else tossed from an open window
or thrown through glass, eaten by gravel or hard earth—I
would not die in water, not that.

✦   ✦   ✦

Fourteen, fifteen, sixteen. The cemetery was where they
went on weekends, a procession of cars like any other there,
or almost, a file of them cutting slow through the markers to
the end of one of the paths. I knew what they did by what they
left behind: pull-tabs, lipsticks and condom wrappers, sometimes a cassette tape—artifacts, shards at a dig. The grounds-
keepers came early on Sundays to collect the evidence, to
rake and pick for the after-church crowd, for me. It took
some looking to find what they missed, but I was exacting,
choosing to walk home after my parents left in the car, mov-

ing on the edges of the paths, an archaeologist in a dark blue dress.

I could've cracked open the plastic shells of cassettes, wound the tape around my sister's stone, a shiny black bunting above a small pyre of cigarette butts, lipsticked and swollen with dew and everything I didn't yet know, the ribbons of music reflecting silently under the bright cold sun.

+　　✦　　+

Sixteen. A carload of boys pulled up next to me on my way to school, just beyond sight of my house and the pool behind my house. They leaned out of the windows, no longer scraped and clumsy—ropy muscles, white skin, long pretty fingers drumming the side of the door. They would spend their weekends in the cemetery, practicing to be grown, to be dead.

There she is, they said, *that's the one, the one who thinks she's too fucking good.*

This was what I had been listening for, the truth of things.

In the street beyond my house I stepped, long steps, mother-may-I steps, moving closer to them than I had ever been.

"No," I said. "That is not what I think at all."

I knew better than to turn and run, or even look behind me. Lot's wife turned to salt, stone-frozen for one look back.

+　　✦　　+

I have forgotten nothing, not the slow burn of whiskey in the back of my throat or the white light of hospital rooms where the death was pumped out of me. Two daughters, one, one-half—my mother fighting to keep me with her long after my father had given up, his closet emptied and his car packed in the space of a day and an envelope of cash on the dining room table, and me at my bedroom window, my mother with her arms around my waist dragging me back inside.

One daughter, one-half, one-fourth—my mother took the lock off the bathroom door after finding me bled white on the tile like an angelfish, my fins gone dry and brittle, my gills like rice paper. No water could pull me under its surface, no current would keep me from floating.

+   +   +

The tricks of memory—there are times when I doubt my-self, when I doubt the veracity of what I know, depending on where you ask me to look. I was returned to my mother after some months, but my sense of this time is gone, distorted, stretched like taffy in a child's hands. I was fed and kept wound tight in blankets, bathed and bandaged up like some-thing fixed. There was no parade of visitors, no boys for me then—flat on your back is not enough, not when there are girls with arms like wings and candied mouths waiting for them like nurses. And there are always girls like that.

+   +   +

I am here, now, a small house at the edge of a small town with drugstore, post office, hardware store, grocery, gas station, produce stand, and houses lining out from there until you get to this one, the last on a street that gives out to mile markers and dried cattails siding a stretch of crumbling state road. From the windows on the second floor you can see out past the backyard and across the field to the spiral slope of an off-ramp. There are no trees to obstruct this view, not behind this house. It is best only to look from the corners of your eyes. To look straight on, unblinking, is unbearable. The gray light of dawn is no different from dusk; the expanse of this sky is too wide.

There are no curtains yet and boxes are still stacked on the floor, the flaps of some laid open to bite your shins in the dark.

I have remembered the close dark of a cardboard cave, crayoned sides, my sister's breath, veins of light that caught an arm not pulled securely in. The sides bulged and grew soft at the seams. She reinforced them with masking tape, a patient carpenter in midsummer. She held the flashlight and I drew windows, a door. I drew myself, her. I drew our clothes magenta and azure and marigold. We smelled of chlorine and coconut.

Now, I blame my mother no more than I blame myself. We were both young then.

OTHER WATER

The man in the house next door is finished dying. I think it must have happened last night, while we were sleeping, because this morning the hearse was there, in front of his house. I looked through the blinds. I have never met him and have no reason to show my face. James tells me that his wife has been gone for days.

By nighttime the door to his house stands open, and cars line the street on either side, fenders close to touching, the wheels of some on lawns, but the neighbors don't complain. They leave their own houses to go to his, carrying covered platters or grocery bags held long-ways, balanced on their forearms, and the hearse, the doctored limousine, is still there.

Where James lives, they keep the deceased in the house for the days before the funeral, and they keep the doors propped open.

+   +   +

When my father died, I was not there to watch. We had not spoken for years by then, my mother speaking for us over variable distances, calling me at the place my husband had taken me to. It was because of my husband that we did not speak, my father and I, though there was no real reason for it. Perhaps by then, by the time our silence was established, my father was already sick, his mind accordioned, the reason falling away like chips of scraped paint. My mother led him from my wedding reception to their car, the last time I saw him walk. My husband was an older man, and mostly kind.

My mother told me, in the months before, that she had put a bed in their living room, a narrow hospital bed with retractable metal sides and an L-shaped rolling tray to fit over it. On the tray, except at mealtimes, were bottles of pills and folded towels, a kidney-shaped receptacle, a toothbrush, the plastic pitcher and nursery intercom.

Although he could no longer navigate the stairs, my father had all of his teeth. She clipped his nails for him while he slept so he would not hurt himself. She picked the small moons of them from the blanket.

Nights, my mother told me, she heard the rattle of the metal bars through the intercom and would go downstairs to check. Once she found him on the floor, his feet in white cotton socks still tangled in the blankets, trying to crawl beneath the bed. She coaxed him out, whispering to him in Italian, her hand on his back. She moved the bed against the wall and got him back into it, and the next day brought boxes from the garage, heavy with Christmas ornaments, to stack in the space between bed and floor. She stacked and wedged the boxes, breaking a few, she heard. It was just summer then.

✦   ✦   ✦

While my father died I lived with my husband in a house on what is called *backwater*. If James were to drive there—which he has never done—he would go from the city to the interstate, then off to a divided highway lined on either side with strip malls, movie theaters, and small square houses, the kind called *bungalows* in other places. He would cross a bridge over the bay, toward the peninsula. The drive from there is longer than it should be, longer than it looks on any map. The road on the other side of the bridge is rutted, sided by cornfields and farms, produce stands with honey and preserves, and fat melons. This road goes on through groves of wye oak and willow until the soil becomes too sandy for that, good for not much more than scrub and sea grass, long sharp blades that cut if they catch you wrong. Miles past this, where land gives out to warm still water, is where we lived then, my husband and I, where I still live.

I have practiced for this moment. I have practiced the way I would walk James down past my front porch to the small curve of beach I have, and lead him into the water, and say, *Look. This is the way the water moves in the shoals.*

✦   ✦   ✦

In the early quiet of our house the phone would ring and my mother's voice in my ear was strained, exhausted. "I was too

106

tired to call last night. But your father," she said, and my husband slept on.

I asked if I should come.

"There's no use in that," she said, carefully. "He wouldn't know you if you did."

My father's body shriveled in upon itself, the skin sagging in the creases below his collarbones and the sunken apron of his hips. My mother rolled him from side to side on the hour, rinsing a plastic dish to place beneath his mouth. The pillowcases were the worst, she said, worse than the blankets or the bottom sheet—there were disposable undergarments and a rubber pad for those.

On Sundays, my mother got up early for Mass. She had a neighbor come to sit with my father for the hour she was gone, and when she got home she pressed a paper plate of cookies into the neighbor's hands, or a *frittata* wrapped in foil. After the neighbor left she bathed and dressed my father, helped him from the bed to the sofa, and spread a crocheted afghan over his wasted lap. She opened the door to his brothers and sisters, a steady stream all morning, and set coffee and liqueurs out on the kitchen table, and pastry. They knelt in front of their brother and took his hands in theirs, squeezing, begging, and my father moved his head from side to side in the manner of a blind man.

I was excused from these preparatory rituals, my presence, if I had been there, superfluous. There was no need for another child, another wife.

What James has never done is left a place. The house where he lives now is only miles from the one where he was born,

and when he speaks to me of leaving I listen only long enough
so he believes that I am.

He says, "I would like to go west," or "I would like to go
to Mexico. I've always wanted to go to Mexico."

But I think that all he *wants* are small things.

For instance, he does not want me. When I get into his bed
at night he slides close, his head in the hollow of my neck, his
feet well under mine, and sleeps. I have never asked for more
than this.

+　　+　　+

After my mother's phone calls, my husband drew me to him.
Don't worry, little bird, he would say, *it will be over soon.*

My husband, then, old and generous, would make love to
me in silence, his face turned away to the water outside our
window.

+　　+　　+

I have seen other water besides this: the Pacific, the Gulf of
Mexico, the Tyrhennian Sea. The Tyrhennian is blue-green,
clear to the rocks that shore it against Amalfi and muddy farther north toward Naples. On our honeymoon, my husband
and I drove south from there along the coast in a tiny shriek-
ing car with a plastic fan affixed to the windshield. We parked
the car in Amalfi to walk the narrow streets, canted at a dangerous angle and bordered by small houses of white and yellow set on crumbling stone steps cut into the side of the cliffs.
We threw our bodies back for balance, our faces up to the sky.
The town smelled of lemons, salt and fish.

We went from Amalfi to Pompeii under the ruinous sun of July. There were lizards on the cracked earth, darting into crevices between the stones that lined the streets. The glare of sun on pumice was blinding.

Stone, everything: the slabs of walls left standing, the partitions of rooms, the shards of pottery. At the entrance to the city was a glass-fronted building, thick-walled and dark. On tables there were stone utensils, stone bowls, a stone dog, legs outstretched, white and porous, and next to it a man, limbs drawn in tight around his body. It would not take long to die like that.

I became faint in the heat and had to sit, head between my knees, while my husband went to get me water.

He was generous with me until the end. He was not like James. If my husband's neighbor had died, he would have been at the house, taking the packages that people brought, putting them in the refrigerator or out on the table. He would have had me take their coats. James keeps his distance—a quiet one, contained by the boundaries of his lawn and mailbox.

I told him this morning to go there, to take some flowers from the yard, or a berry pie.

"I am leaving soon," I said.

+   +   +

My husband and I trolled for crabs. Trolling is this: a hundred-yard rope knotted every few feet with pieces of eel that have been packed in brine to keep. The rope is wound on a pulley-wheel and mounted on the stern, then let out, bit by bit, into the bay. My husband steered—captained. He doubled the boat back along the rope while I stood on a platform on the bow, net in hand, and leaned to scoop the crabs that came up to the eel to feed. These I tossed, scrabbling, into a bushel.

You have to go out beyond the shoals for crabs like these, to the deepest part of the inlet—eight feet, here, is deep. Just before dusk, in the space of an hour or so, we could go home with half a bushel, shells seven inches from tip to tip. The going rate on the mainland for crabs like these—ninety, a hundred dollars a bushel, depending.

When my husband told me he was leaving he was kind even then, holding my shoulders like I was some fragile thing.

"The house will be yours. I'm too old for all this," he gestured out, sweeping in the room and the porch and the sliver of beach beyond and bringing his hand back to rest on my sunburnt shoulder.

I was the one to net the crabs, to put up the tomatoes and preserves. My hands were rough, sometimes scalded, and my feet cut by shells and glass.

✦   ✦   ✦

At my father's funeral, my mother gave me pictures she had taken of him before he died. There is little you can see in the photos: an old man, frail, wrapped in blankets on the couch, but nothing more than that. She told me she had tried to show him the postcards I sent from Italy, to show him how close I was to home. There were some things I told her, about the amazing heat, the fishmarkets. She nodded, remembering.

She told me that my father had hit her only once in all their years of marriage. She was bathing him, she said, lifting up his arms and sponging beneath them, squeezing the water into a basin on the rolling tray. He became excited and began to thrash, his arms pinwheeling, knocking the sponge from her hand and the basin to the floor of the living room, and as she turned to pick it up he caught her on the side of her face with his knuckles. She did not say if she had fallen. When she went to see his doctor the next day she covered the bruise with heavy makeup. This happened while I was away.

She told me this on the way home from the graveyard. She said, "If your father knew he did that he would have cried."

+   ✦   +

James has no idea how far my house is, the time it takes to get there. I have asked for nothing. I have taught him how to garden, how not to plant the seeds too deep. I have told him about Naples, about the crescent bay and the Gulf of Salerno that runs between the mainland and Capri.

On Capri, my husband left me sitting at the table of a cafe while he went to make a call. The phone was behind the counter and he stood there, speaking into it, sipping Campari.

On the table in front of me was a plate of *carpaccio* with olive oil and cracked pepper. This was the sort of thing he ordered for me.

When the boy came in he ran straight to me, shouting in a mix of English and Italian, plucking at my sleeves with small dark hands. His eyes were shining. *Street*, I understood, *come*, and *please*. I looked to the back of the cafe as he pulled me from my chair. My husband saw and motioned toward me, *Go, go.* The boy pulled me up and out into the sunlight.

Around the corner he swung me into a group of them, boys not much older than he was, fifteen at the most, and they circled me, laughing and spitting, speaking only in English then, the boy who had come for me saying, *Where's your Papa now, huh, huh, the old man he left you, gave you to me,* and they closed in, grabbing for my hair, my shoes, pulling off my shoes and pressing me against the stone wall of the cafe to crush their skinny bodies on me, to reach up under my skirt for the stockings I was not wearing on that hot day. And it did not occur to me to wonder, until much later, after they had run, whom my husband was speaking to, or if my father ever thought of this place that was so close to his home.

Do you find it difficult to believe, that such things happen?

✦　✦　✦

After my father's funeral, I sat for coffee with my mother. The hospital bed was gone from the living room; drivers from the rental place had come to pick it up the day before. The boxes of ornaments were still stacked against the wall, some corners crushed flat, the only trace of what had been there.

I left her in her husband's house to drive back to mine. You can smell the way the air changes, the farther you go.

✦　✦　✦

People come to the house next door for three days. The flowers are beginning to spill out onto the porch—baskets of ferns, wreaths, chrysanthemums in pots wrapped with col-

ored foil. The ceremony of death is an ordered one, its movements slow and courteous, its trappings contained in baskets,
on covered plates and silk-lined coffins. There is nothing for
a stranger to do.

I say, "I am leaving here tomorrow."

In bed, James draws me to him, his hands impossibly soft,
and folds himself into sleep.

+   +   +

In Amalfi, the water is far from wherever you stand, hundreds
of feet below the houses and orchards, foaming low against
the rocks. The boys there stand wide-legged on the over-
hangs, throwing figs into the sea or at the girls on the docks
below. You can, if you are careful, slide along these ledges on
your stomach, your face turned down to the water and the
spray above it.

At my house, the water moves quietly in the shoals. I sleep
with the windows open in the wide bed my husband left,
where James has never been—*how is it that a man can leave
everything behind?*

I ask you this—you, who have never left.

In my dreams I swim, and when I wake I am surprised to
find myself dry. I dream of the Tyrhennian, and know that the
boys there mean no harm.

THE GIFT

Her hands, then, were small, thin and bony, shiny with fish guts and stuck with scales and kissed even so by the women, whose own hands were spotted and old. Her stinking hands, knuckles cracked, palms cut and punctured by crab shells, were seized over the cold run-off behind the counter where the fish were hosed down and kissed by the women whose names were Carmella and Lucia and Theresa. Carmella and Lucia and Theresa wound kerchiefs around their heads and had known her grandmother when her grandmother had rolled up her sleeves to lean off her own father's boat and hauled dripping nets of fish up and over the side of the boat, thrashing at her bare callused feet.

They kissed her hands.

"Sophie, Sophie," they said, "you have a gift, a gift from God in these hands."

Sophie gutted the fish and cleaned the shrimp. From six in

the morning she cleaned the shrimp till noon at least, depending on the number of bushels and the lines of women waiting at the counter, shifting from foot to foot in the damp early morning, clutching sticky wrinkled lists in their hands. She stood at the stainless steel sink behind the display cases, hose in one hand, small knife in the other, a row of wooden baskets on the floor in front of her with fish, clams, and oysters, crabs if they were lucky. But it was always the shrimp the women wanted, especially on a Saturday, and so this bushel she hoisted first onto the counter and hosed, mud and sea grass washing into the gutter against the tiled wall. And then the knife, balanced loose in the last three fingers of her hand—with her thumb and index finger she peeled and cleaned, tail then legs then a flip and twist of shell off the back and the knife down the center, her thumb dragging the vein. To her right the pile of shrimp grew, gray and shining.

They were sorted, weighed, priced, spread on the ice of the case, and garnished with lemon and parsley. And then there were the olives.

"Sophie," Lucia said, squeezing and kissing her red stinking hands, "you are the only one to trust for my olives."

Sophie prepared the olives. Slick with oil, they were pitted and thrown in a wooden bowl and tossed with peppers, celery, spices, and garlic, and stored to marinate overnight before being sold the next day, six dollars a pound. They would have been heavier, but the customers liked them pitted, the easier to stab with cellophane-tipped toothpicks. Nicer for parties, they said.

These were the things that Sophie did, and at the end of the day she walked home from the market. In the street the smell of rain came up from the gutters.

✦   ✦   ✦

Her grandmother stood on the boat: bare feet, strong arms, sweat beaded along her hairline, caught in the dark soft fuzz above her lip. Sixteen, no older than that. In the boat also were Sophie's great-grandfather and his younger brother Joseph, who wore a leather cap with a green braid around the brim.

This was the photo on Sophie's dresser, the two men and her grandmother, who was called Carrie, an American girl's name, until the day she died. In this photo that Joseph's wife took, Sophie's great-grandfather sits, hands on knees, his face shadowed by the brim of his cap, but Joseph's cap is far enough back so that his face is clear and wide, bright like the water beneath them and shining, and his hand is on Carrie's shoulder, on the bare curve of skin and strong bone. Sophie, squinting, saw his fingers beneath her grandmother's strap of dress, beneath his niece's strap, his fingers there on the salt and sweat of her skin in the wide bright sunlight, caught blurry in the lens held by his wife's unsteady hand.

✦   ✦   ✦

Sophie walked at night, keeping to the outside of the sidewalks on her way home, away from the shadowed doors and alleyways, past the row houses with brick steps and wrought iron railings, windows above boxes spilling over with small pale flowers, wilted only at the edges. In the still air was the smell of rain from the day and the sound of her voice, humming, tuneless.

In her house she ate. There was a roast that she ate with her fingers so that the meat tasted of fish. Friday night had been a casserole of baked macaroni that had tasted of fish as well, a fish-taste that somehow managed to make its way from her fingers to the fork to her food. So this Saturday night she did not bother with the fork. When she finished she washed the plate and left it in the drainer and scrubbed her face and hands. She kept an aloe plant in the kitchen and each night broke off a piece and rubbed it over her knuckles and palms and fingers till they glistened. She clenched and unclenched her hands, felt the stick and pull of the aloe in the creases of her palms, and was amazed that she could move her hands this way, the fingers at random, waving at nothing in the air, holding nothing, *doing* nothing. They were her own again in the uselessness of their movements. They would not be kissed, soaped and dried and lotioned as they were.

✦ ✦ ✦

The story Sophie's grandmother told was this:

She had come to the United States on a boat at age twelve, met by relatives in Rhode Island and taken to an American house and given dinner and a bath and a bed. The next morning she was packed on a train to Baltimore with her name pinned to her shirt and a piece of paper in her hand with her Uncle Joseph's name and address on it. Carrie had spoken no English. When she arrived in Baltimore she stood on the platform at the edge of the steps that led to the main concourse of the terminal. She stood with her bags between her legs, refusing to move, refusing to go to the bathroom though she was ready to cry and afraid of having an accident. She stood this way until the platform cleared and she saw a man, a boy still, really, holding the hat with the braid that she remembered from her father's house in the mountains above Naples.

"*Zio!*" she cried, and waved the piece of paper over her head.

Joseph, then, was not yet twenty.

He took her home with him to the rooms above the grocery store he ran with his wife. They made a bed for her on the floor of the pantry and she worked in the grocery store and waited for her father to follow.

This was the beginning of the story that Sophie's grandmother told. She lived with her father and slept under her dead mother's linens in the room next to her Uncle Joseph and his wife. She learned English and got a job in the spice factory on the other side of the harbor. Still, in the mornings she took the boat out with her father and Joseph and sometimes Joseph's wife and hauled up the muddy shellfish. She married Sophie's grandfather at twenty-two. She kept her job at the factory but moved with her husband to a room in a different block. She gave birth to Sophie's four aunts and finally Sophie's father, and she kept her job until she was forced to retire. That is the rest of the story, the story she told in her cracked English until the day she died.

What she did not tell Sophie, or anyone else as far as Sophie knew, was the story of Joseph's hand on her shoulder, his fingers pressing the brown skin until he marked it red, until he rubbed the smells of salt and fish into the cheap cotton of her dress, until Sophie could almost see these marks in the blurred and ancient photo she took from her father's album, until she could smell the brine in the creases of the paper.

✦   ✦   ✦

Sophie, on a Sunday morning, lay in a bed that was not hers, the first such bed since she had crawled into her mother's bed as a child and listened to her father snore from across the room and breathed her mother's warm smell in the dark of the blankets, a smell of oil and flour—the first bed not her own since then. She lay in this bed in its empty room, walls bare but for a mirror, no crucifix hanging above it, the floor polished wood, gleaming dully in the gray October light.

She lay in her lover's bed.

She lay next to her lover, who at the market had paid with hundred dollar bills and apologized for having nothing smaller.

He had watched her, she knew, for months, watched her early on the Saturday mornings when he came with a list and stood in line with the women. But he did not shift, impatient, on the balls of his feet, on the heels of his expensive leather shoes. He watched her as she moved through the scaly bloody runoff behind the counter, his eyes pale and distant, as though she were a picture in an old magazine, edges wrinkled, corners dog-eared. She felt his eyes tracking her, his gaze like cold water raising shivers on her arms, but her face was hot, her lips dry. The day he became her lover the knife slipped and she cut herself.

She screamed, though this was not something she did; on the rare occasions when the knife slipped she simply rinsed her hand and wrapped it in gauze and brown paper and carried on. The scars were nothing. They belonged to the quick brilliant mindlessness of her hands.

This time she screamed and dropped the knife, and Theresa was there, murmuring *felia, felia,* and holding her hand under the faucet. When Sophie looked up the women in line were staring, wondering, she thought, if any of her blood had touched the food. The man in whose bed she would lie was gone, his absence blinding, and in a matter of hours she would lie splayed and tangled in her clothes in his empty room, this man for whom she had weighed out olives, this man who had made her bleed before he'd ever touched her.

+   ✦   +

After the first time, Sophie had knelt in church and asked to be forgiven. She bowed her head before the altar, her hair matted and still smelling of the boy who had been her first, smelling of him and of the cracked vinyl of his car , and she thought of the confessions she had made as a child. *Forgive me Father, I have lied. I have been disrespectful to my parents. I have taken the Lord's name in vain.*

All that was nothing, even as a child she had known it was nothing, and still she hated the tiny box of the confessional, the darkness that smelled of sweat and grief and the stale denture breath of the old who had been there before her.

Her grandmother had waited for her in a pew by the altar. She waited for Sophie to come and kneel and say her penance. From the corner of her eye Sophie could see the rosary draped through the bent fingers, the crystal sparkling blue and gold in the dusty afternoon light, brighter by far than the diamond chip in the wedding band that her grandfather had slipped onto his wife's finger when she had been called Carrie. The rosary dripped and ran through her grandmother's fingers as the water must have done, graceful, effortless.

After the penance was finished, her grandmother took her for a shaved ice or a lemon stick, and when they got home, Sophie asked her for the rosary, and her grandmother's eyes filled with tears. *"Nipote, nipote mia,"* she said, and pulled Sophie to her and laid the rosary in her small smooth hand.

In her room, Sophie had sat in front of the mirror with her Communion veil on her head, listening for her grandmother's footsteps in the hall, fingering the cut crystal beads as she did in church but without words or thoughts of words, without prayer or supplication for intercession or forgiveness. She stared into the mirror until her eyes were glazed and the reflection of her mouth was an indistinct blur in the glass. She thought, *I haven't done anything wrong.*

But she had, and what she had done wrong was nothing simple enough for her to name. She sat at the table during Sunday dinners and bowed her head while her father said the prayer in Italian, but she did not pray along. Instead, she watched her mother's lips moving silently above her folded hands, nails broken to the quicks and bitten until the cuticles bled. She watched her grandmother next to her, cheeks caved and hollow, praying aloud, always a syllable or two ahead of Sophie's father, as if she were racing him to the end, to the finish line, as though there were something at the end of the prayer, something more than baked chicken or *past e fagiole*, as though when the prayer were over God Himself would appear at the table to sweep them all up into heaven. As though there were something, something no less than salvation.

And if God had appeared, Sophie thought, they would all be taken except for her. He knew that she hated these dinners, hated the prayers in Italian that her friends would laugh at if she had ever asked them to stay, hated the tomato sauce ladled over everything, even the chicken, even the fish, so that her blouses all were spattered with it. Even with bleach the stains never came out, not completely, they simply faded into yellowish ideograms. Sometimes at night she couldn't sleep and called for her mother, and her mother brought her a glass of water and told her to say the rosary and not to forget the Mysteries, that it was good to fall asleep praying. But God knew that Sophie only got through a decade before she lost her place, because there were no beads to count on. And so she reached under the blankets, under her nightgown, and her hand on her own skin felt as though it were not her own, not attached to her body, and she thought, *God can see me doing this,* and was ashamed, although she did not know why.

She never confessed that.

+   ✦   +

Sophie's lover, the day he became her lover, paid her in the morning and in the evening stood waiting at the entrance to the market. She was not surprised. Her hand was bandaged, stiff and awkward, and he held the door for her.

"You must do that often," he said, gesturing, and Sophie waited.

"The cut, I mean," he said. "Does it hurt?"

His eyes were pale, lighter even than they had seemed at a distance, pale enough to Sophie that she wondered if the light was awful for him, if he saw her in a brilliant white haze like sun on water, if he saw her at all.

"Not often," she said. She did not want to talk to him. She had nothing to say. But she knew that she would go with him to his house or apartment, or if not there to somewhere else. There were places for people like her to go, places like the room above the grocery store where Carrie had slept before she was Sophie's grandmother, where she had heard Joseph and his wife in the room next to hers, where she had fallen asleep listening to them and maybe reciting the rosary in her head.

Sophie's lover, whose name she did not know, took her to the apartment with its empty rooms and polished floors, and led her through a maze of unpacked boxes. At the end of the maze was the bed, and she lay on it and waited for him to undress her. His hands were under her shirt, tugging at her bra, trying to get everything off at once, clumsy, pulling hard and uselessly. She tried to do it herself, before he tore a seam or popped a button, thinking to help, to make it go faster, but he took her hands and pulled them back and down. She heard the creak of her shoulder blades and felt her hand opening and the seep of blood in her palm.

"Don't help me," he said, catching her wrists tight against the small of her back, "don't help me," he said, "don't move."

I gutted fish for you, she thought, and he pushed her skirt to her waist and propped her hips with a pillow. He hooked his fingers into her underwear and yanked them aside, and if she had known that there would be this pillow and this empty room she would have spit on him. That morning she would have said, *There is not one thing you can teach me. I could cut you open, I could gut you as you stand there. I know how.*

✦   ✦   ✦

Sunday mornings there was the smell of pigs being slaughtered across the harbor. In her head this Sunday was the sound of Lucia's voice, *Oh, Sophie, the olives are so wonderful today.* Sophie crossed the empty park and squeezed through a hole in the chain link fence behind her house.

She had left him sleeping in the bed.

She had dressed barefoot in the cold of the bedroom, left her shoes off until she had got out of the building, the cracked sidewalk catching at her socks.

She had left a smear of blood on the pillow, dried brown, moon-shaped, and on the floor by the bed were shreds of paper towel.

So wonderful, Sophie.

She had left him with his legs spread wide, one foot hanging from the side of the bed, veins blue, muscles ropy, skin paper-white and thin, and she had stared at his foot for a moment before leaving, stared at the strange pale sole of it, white and almost bloodless, not callused or blistered or swollen. His face was hidden in the pillow.

He was not the first, not even close to the first who groped at her buttons or zippers that stuck. The feel of his hands on her skin was not new to her, not new at all except for the softness of them and the coolness.

Sophie stood that morning at her back door with the smell of the pigs and the squeals, low, distant and shrill, and she imagined the hot damp of the slaughtering room in the plant across the water, the coppery closeness of that room beneath the chill of the wind. She stood with her hand on the knob of her back door and wondered at what she had done.

+   ✦   +

Uncle Joseph had died soon after Carrie's wedding to Sophie's grandfather, before the first child was born. He had died in a way not unusual for a man in his position, a man with a small store that did not always do well, a man with debts that he settled during card games in the rooms behind the grocery, a man who could barely speak English. He was beaten, and died, and was buried, was grieved. That was the moment, Sophie imagined, that her grandmother had become her grandmother, before any of her children were born or married or had children of their own. That is the story that Sophie knew.

She lay in her bed on that Sunday afternoon, bathed, lotioned, smelling of the talc she'd put under her arms and between her legs. She lay in her nightgown under heavy blankets, blinds drawn, windows open, and on the street below
was the sound of footsteps, of children crying and parents
scolding. Families walked to the market for the Sunday
brunch that they would eat at counters or standing around
the high wooden tables set up in the aisles between the stalls,
the brunch that they had been thinking of as their stomachs
growled during the long sermons they'd sat through. The seafood stall was closed on Sundays so Carmella and Lucia and
Theresa could go to Mass with their own families, then come
home and lay out the food for the children and grandchildren
who came for the Sunday visits, for the sons who sat in front
of the television while the daughters-in-law wiped the chins
of the babies.

Sophie lay in her bed and listened to these sounds.

There were the four of them in those small rooms, Joseph
and his wife and Carrie and her father, the two men barely
speaking, because Joseph was young and brash and too free
with the little money they had. Carrie's father knew his
youngest brother, knew the tilt of the leather cap with the
sweat-stained brim, angled back from his forehead so he
could peer through the longish dark hair, so he could smile
and wink at the women who came into the grocery as he
handed peppermint sticks to their daughters. He gave them
the two-cent peppermint sticks free, and their mothers
blushed and giggled like girls, and talked to each other over
the washing about Joseph at the grocery store, the only man

on his block without a mustache, so young and charming, so good with the children, so sad he had none himself. But they prayed for the wife every day: a man like that needed children of his own.

Carrie's father, then, was already old, his wife dead, his other daughters grown, gone, one to Rome and the others higher up into the mountains above Naples, so that when he looked at his youngest child his voice shriveled and died in his throat. There was nothing for him to say: he had forgotten the words, and the forgetting was complete. He remembered that he was Carrie's father, and he remembered the quickness of Joseph's fingers on the farm, with the fences and the bales and later the fish hauled up so quickly, those fingers so quickly brushing Carrie's ankles as he leaned past her to grab the dripping net.

He remembered all this as he lay in bed under the quilt his wife had made, the pieces of misshapen fabric faded now but still stitched tight, hands fast on his wooden rosary. In the next room were the sounds of Joseph and his wife, and in the next bed was his daughter.

Sixteen, seventeen, Carrie was old enough so that the women in the neighborhood asked when she would be married, when her father would make the announcement. Old enough so that at night she listened and tried not to sleep before the sounds in the next room stopped, the rustling and creaking that made her face go hot and red, and the voices, the breathless voice of her uncle especially, of _Zio_.

Call me Joseph, he had said, _I'm not much older than you._

One night she got up, _for water,_ she would have told her father if he had woken. She got up and went to the basin, and from the doorway saw the edge of their bed, the sheet crumpled, one edge dragging on the floor. From the washstand in the doorway she could see the pile of sheets and on top of them Joseph's foot and bare calf. The ball of his foot was braced against the bed frame, his leg tense, stretched, quivering. Carrie turned to her father's doorway and stood, staring, watching her father's heavy sleep beneath the quilt her mother had made. She stood until she heard Joseph's long exhale, until she could almost feel the hot whistle of his breath against her back. She stood until she heard his tread on the floorboards as he got up to get some water. Even then she did not move. He passed behind her and she did not move. She heard the drip of water in the basin, the ladle against the heavy porcelain bowl, and still she stood, watching her father sleep as her uncle moved naked behind her.

She did not turn.

She would not have turned, Sophie knew, even when she felt Joseph's hand against the small of her back, at the narrow dip of it, even when she felt the warm damp of his hand through her nightgown, the wet of it on her shoulder blades and down the length of her spine, still straight, the knobs of vertebrae still aligned. She would not have turned when she felt the hand cupping one hip, small yet, a hip that would fit in the palm of a big man's hand, a hip not wide and creaking yet with the weight of children. It would have been impossible for her to turn and face him, or to run and wake her father: her body would not move, crumbled as it was into skin and nerve and flesh and bone, nothing more or less than those things. Carrie would have stood until Joseph lifted the hand from her body and went back to his wife, shut the door and pinched the candle, and still Carrie would have stood, her nightgown drying on her back.

Sophie had not wished, neither asked nor prayed, to see these things, and yet the images appeared before her eyes, more vivid than the street in front of her as she walked to work or as the gleaming wet fish spread still twitching on the counters at the market, more vivid than the walls of her bedroom where she lay before sleep. This girl, this Carrie, had bones and flesh more solid than her own, had skin brighter, softer. There was only the beginning of the story in the pictures, only hints and whispers. Finally, there was the end, the end of the bright smooth skin, cracked and weathered until it peeled away in papery shreds to rest on her grandmother's shoes.

Oh, Sophie, your hands!

Sophie lay in bed, the blankets drawn tight to her throat against the gray Sunday morning. Before Carrie's skin had stretched and faded, before she had lain in her husband's bed, she had been touched, first in a darkened hallway in front of her sleeping father, and then again, and again, fleeting brushes in the boat or the grocery until Carrie could not see him without her stomach roiling into knots as she prayed, *Please help me, he is my father's brother.*

He had touched her until the words were gone from her head, until she sat mute in church between the men and waited for the store to close and her father to sleep and Joseph to step out into the hall and wait for her to come to him while his wife lay silently in their bedroom.

Sophie, you have a gift.

Carrie, Carrie on the boat, legs spread, braced, muscles knotted and wet and lovely—to Joseph she was priceless, or perhaps not, perhaps simply a thing to covet and seize when his brother tipped his hat over his eyes for a nap in the sun.

Legs spread, muscles tight, Joseph's long fingers around her ankle then moving up her leg, warm beneath the damp cotton of her skirt then hot. Carrie stood rocking in the sun as the fish flipped and thrashed at her feet, and Sophie clenched her fists and waited as something she could not quite see moved toward her, smelling of fish, breath whistling like the breath of the pigs in the slaughterhouse. She waited for it to come and draw her eyes closed.

Carrie's arms and legs and smooth brown throat, her hair drawn back, her father sleeping behind her, her uncle awake, so wide awake, her husband not even waiting for her yet—Carrie, then, could have walked on water.

WHAT IS CLOSE

In traveling Susan is light, her body stretched to touch each place she's been. She is a careful driver, but fast. She keeps to the interstates, willingly giving up what other people call *scenery* for speed and what it brings: the change in temperature on a southerly route, the dip of red sun on a westerly one. The particular, the exclusive—towns, storefronts, cornfields, signposts that say "welcome" or "come again"—this is what she does not want. What drives her forward is the space between, the not-there, the neither. In the car she is weightless, lost, her voice swallowed in wind.

The last place she leaves is a large house crowded by palm trees, live oak, bougainvillea trellises—lush and horrible, surrounded by swampland. The night before leaving she sleeps on a couch in the living room, where French doors open onto the deck outside, dreaming of what might come in while her eyes are closed. Perhaps a lizard, perhaps only rain.

When she leaves, she drives north. To her right is the Atlantic, and the moon comes up.

+ ✦ +

When Susan was six, she was sent from their island. Her mother became sick, though she realizes now that this *becoming* had taken a long time, longer than she knew then. On the endless drive to the mainland, the city, to her grandparents' house, her father explained that her mother would be in the hospital for a time and then back home. He would be caring for her, for weeks, possibly a month or more, and so it would be better for her to spend the summer in the city with her grandparents, and with their neighbors, the cousins she saw only rarely. Although he would try to visit her, her father said, steering, glancing more frequently into the rearview mirror as the traffic thickened, she should not be upset if he didn't, *couldn't*, come. His time would be taken up. And when she came back at the end of the summer, in time for school, her mother would be back to normal—this was the word he used, *normal*. She remembers precisely because of what normal, for her mother, was: stiff hands, white circles around her eyes, fisted mouth.

At her grandparents' her father helped her from the car, carrying her bag and pillow down the alley behind their block and through the narrow strip of yard, mostly concrete but edged with the rosebushes her grandmother coaxed up— yellow and blush-pink blooms, delicate and only vaguely scented—and down the steep well of steps into their cellar kitchen. She would realize later that the drive was not so long as it had seemed, less than two hours in the car, alone with her father, the world outside flying too fast for memory. Her father stayed for a cup of coffee with his wife's parents. Her grandfather poured Susan a cup, too, half-coffee and half-milk, with sugar, and listened as her father recited her mother's hospitalization schedule.

He finished his coffee and kissed his daughter on the head, already driving, already gone. Neither of her grandparents drove. They spoke to Susan's mother every day on the phone, and though Susan's father had said that this might be impossible for the next few weeks, it was not.

Some years later, after her grandparents died, she learned that it had been a hysterectomy. Her mother had only been thirty-four, and from there she seemed to age exponentially with every passing year, her lips thinner, skin looser, her walk clumsy and uncertain, until the fast fall, the slipping into something slack and ugly, the finish.

That summer Susan was left to play with her cousins Bobby and JoJo. There is evidence of this, a photo she found much later in her grandmother's night stand, which she was cleaning out before the funeral, looking for something—a pin, medal, rosary—something to lay in the coffin by her grandmother's powdered hand.

In the photo she and Bobby and JoJo are in a small plastic pool, Bobby and JoJo on either side of her, all of them squinting and smiling into the lens. The boys are nine and five to her six, but they are both much bigger than she is, obvious even from their shoulders up. She is wearing a yellow two-piece bathing suit that she remembers well, orange flowers appliquéd on the straps. Behind the pool are the rose-bushes.

They played in the basement of her grandparents' house that summer, in the rooms behind the kitchen. There was a bucket of seashells in a closet there, collected on the beach in Atlantic City where Susan and her parents had gone some years before. She did not—still doesn't—remember this trip, but she knows that she was disturbed by the shells, symmetrical, rinsed, and dried hospital-white. They were not like the shells she found on the beach in front of the house where she lived with her parents, broken, some jagged, pink and purple and gray, washed up with bits of glass worn smooth by water. These were clean, colorless, and perfect.

But these white shells were in a bucket, and there were brushes and watercolors, and she was happy enough to paint them and leave them to dry on paper towels on the floor, happy to do this one Sunday after church while her grandmother cooked and her grandfather sat in a bar up the street.

The basement was below street level, and so the windows on the wall behind her were high up, flush with the sidewalk outside, and from these windows in front of the house she heard horns honking, the backfiring of trucks, shouts, and occasionally a can bouncing from the concrete to the screens. From the kitchen she heard meat sizzling in a pan and a low radio, and smelled chicken, bread crumbs, and oregano. She painted the shells and turned on the television, flipping the dial till she found a baseball game.

She passed the afternoon like this and her grandmother

found her, saying "Honey, turn off the TV, now, and come outside to the yard. I have to go get your grandfather. Miss Hazel will keep an eye on you for a minute."

Older now, memory bright and fierce, she was glad to have recalled that the phrase was *your goddamn grandfather.* She was glad to have remembered the resigned and unwavering love her grandmother kept for her husband, half-drunk often, singing, pinching his wife on the rear as she served him his food, sometimes reaching to squeeze her breast and wink at his granddaughter across the table as his wife slapped and cursed him, laughing, and Susan looked on, eyes wide in amazement.

She sat on the strip of grass in the backyard, sure that Miss Hazel could see her every move, watching for her grandparents to appear at the mouth of the alley. Her painted shells were drying on their paper towels, the chicken warm under a dishcloth in the kitchen.

She kept close to Miss Hazel because the boys were playing farther down the alley, throwing baseballs against the aluminum siding of garage doors and often over them to bounce two, three, four times across the roofs of the garages and sometimes even over the top of the warehouse behind them. The older ones could throw that hard, that far.

"Those damn kids," muttered Miss Hazel, fingering Susan's grandmother's roses.

Bobby and JoJo were among these boys. Susan imagined that if she kept tight and small enough against the wall of the house they would not be able to see her, which perhaps was true. It was also possibly true that they were simply busy with something else that day, that playing with their cousin was a thing reserved for days less interesting.

+ ✦ +

The game they had played the day before was this:

"It's a contest," Bobby said, "to see who gets to be the pitcher. Whoever can drink the most water fastest wins."

The three of them had huddled in the back room of the basement, farthest from the kitchen. There was a washing machine and dryer, a deep laundry sink, and a tiled corner of the floor with a drain and a shower nozzle attached to the wall above it.

"Girls first," Bobby had said, and she began.

She drank from a plastic measuring cup that sat on the back of the sink, filling it with cold water, drinking it down, and filling it again, using both hands as first one and then the other became unsteady. *It's only water*, she remembers thinking now, *it can't hurt me. It's only water, only water.*

She continued drinking until pain settled first between her eyes, then behind them, until she felt the water sloshing sickly inside her. How many cups held under the faucet? She had lost count.

"Don't worry," Bobby said, "I'm keeping track. You next, JoJo."

So JoJo filled the cup as she had done but only sipped from it, swished the water around in his mouth, gargled with it, smiling, and let it run out from between his teeth and down his chin, wetting the front of his shirt.

"This is stupid," she had said. "I'm not playing anymore."
She got up to leave them there, dimly furious, not sure why,
knowing only that she wanted to go to the bathroom and then
lie down on the couch next to her grandfather.

Bobby had grabbed her by the wrist as she stood to leave
and pulled her to the floor, straddling her knees-on-shoul-
ders, and began to bounce, lightly at first, then using more of
his weight, bouncing on her belly and distended bladder
while JoJo stood at her head, laughing, still letting the water
run warm out of his mouth and onto her face.

This went on until Susan had thought she might pass out,
vomit. She refused to scream for her grandfather because
she knew that if she screamed her bladder would let go in a
hot rush, and so she pretended that she *had* no body from
the waist down, no *between-my-legs*. She was nothing but
eyes screwed tight shut and bony shoulders against the ce-
ment until Bobby finally let her up and she half-staggered,
half-crawled to the shower, pulling her shorts and underwear down and squatting over the drain while her cousins
watched.

+   ✦   ✦

At their mother's funeral, many years later, Bobby and JoJo
were pallbearers. She had heard from family that they had
both managed to finish high school before marrying the girls
who were pregnant with their children. Susan was in town
only briefly then, expensive-looking with her smooth hair
and dark dress. Her cousins' mother died a drunk. At the
wake Bobby was serene, squeezing her arm as she kissed his

cheek and offered her condolences. He managed the service bays at a car dealership.

She was standing by the door of the funeral home when JoJo approached her, and what she thought of most after she drove away from there was the vulgar incongruity of his face and body, that big boy in a man's suit, going to fat already, jowly, eyes like chips of glass in a face that had not changed at all, soft beardless cheeks, wet lips.

He wrapped his arms around her, murmured in her ear, "Hey Suze, see my wife in the corner? By the couch?" Their wives stood back from the rest of the family.

Susan stretched to look over his shoulder, still in his arms, and saw a young girl, sullen, pregnant, a Styrofoam cup in her hand.

"Not mine," JoJo whispered, running his big hand down her back, catching the fabric of her dress on his heavy rings, "that kid, shit, not mine——"

She pulled back from him, quickly, not so much to get away as to be able to see his face, because though she thought enough years had passed she wanted to make sure. She stepped back, braced against his upper arms as he tilted forward so that in another place they might have appeared to be dancing.

"Hey, listen," JoJo said, "what are you doing after this? It's been too long, do you maybe want to come for a drink with me? There's a place close, up the street, if you're not——"

The years were in his face, his buried face, eyes glittering with neither meanness nor grief but a desperate good humor, his hands at his sides, feet shuffling, still dancing.

✦　✦　✦

She stops in bars while driving.

West Virginia. The room is large and too brightly lit, showing bare tables with metal chairs, paneled walls, and a scuffed parquet dance floor, empty. The ceiling is low, tiled and stained. She sits at a table in the corner and orders a beer from a waitress with beaded combs in her hair. Because it is not crowded it is easy for her to watch the others watch her— mostly men, denim and dusty boots of indeterminate age, and faces like that. The few women carefully look away from her, any other way.

She drinks her beer and a second appears. The waitress, by way of explanation, nods at a table across the room before setting it down.

She raises the bottle, drinks, and watches the men speak and smile, then laugh.

One approaches when he sees her collecting her things. His eyes are clouded, his skin high polished, fine leather. He sits across from her and rests his arms on the table, palms down, fingers spread.

"I have a place," he says, smiling at her as a doctor might— merciful, benevolent—"and I know you ain't from around here. You look to me like a tri-county piece of tail."

✦　✦　✦

Delaware. The room is open to a deck that faces a marina. In the mid-afternoon light, dusty shadows tumbling down to the planked floor, she is drinking gin.

This is a good place, she thinks, and knows that she is close to home.

The man a few seats down offers her a section of his newspaper and she accepts though she has no real desire to read: an acknowledgment of place, presence, those things she will need when she arrives where she is going.

Juniper, citrus, smoke, and salt, and she opens this paper. *May I have the pleasure?* he has written in black marker on the top of a page, ink bleeding through to the ones behind.

There is no music in the room, only the sound of a small TV turned low, and gulls. *Pleasure*, she thinks. She stands and there is pleasure in that, in the small of her back, now vertical. Gin, lime. *A dance? And another, and more?*

He smiles, teeth bared. She is close to nothing.

✦   ✦   ✦

She was sitting on the front steps of her grandparents' house, thinking about her father, whom she had wanted to call that day. Her grandmother had said to wait, to let her call him first to see how things were going, to arrange a time for him to call back later, possibly after her mother was sleeping.

Her grandmother, Susan knew, was displeased with both her parents, though she could not have said why she thought this was so.

She had a red Popsicle, dessert. It was dusk and she was waiting. Across the street, in the schoolyard, older boys were playing ball. Their girls were watching them, smoking cigarettes. She had told her grandparents that she did not want to play with her cousins anymore.

She could, with concentration, call up her father's voice in her head: *sweetheart*, he called her, and *piper,* like the birds, walking tiny holes through the sand.

She had grown used to the noise and the gray light of dusk. She liked the brick wall of the school, which her grandfather had chalked for her in the way of a hopscotch grid to bounce a ball against. She threw with precision.

The Popsicle was finished. She scraped the wooden stick against the side of the steps, methodically, ten scrapes per edge. This was the way to make a spear.

Two of the boys were fighting. There was the beginning, the pushing and shoving, words she knew already not to say. The girls moved to pull them apart, their movements less graceful than those of the boys who rocked and bounced on the balls of their feet, shoulders loose, hips loose.

The neighbors were beginning to appear, in doorways, on porches, drawn by the shouting in the schoolyard. The boys moved more quickly, with smaller steps, jabbing hands, until the cut flesh of one opened, bloomed, red petalling on his neck by the shoulder. She heard the bright shatter of broken glass, the rest of the bottle hitting the pavement, and then the neighbors—how many at once?—running back inside houses for phones, for help.

The screen door slammed behind her and she was suddenly in her grandfather's arms, the Popsicle stick dropped, lost. He was yelling, it seemed to her, at the girls who were sobbing across the street, as though they were to blame.

Later, years later, she found herself on the beach in front of her parents' house, in the corduroy lap of a boy like these. She opened her mouth willingly for his tongue. He turned her on his lap to face him, wrapped her legs around his waist. Her bare feet dug into cool night sand. She kissed him like this for some length of time, dazzled by the darkness of his hair, and the sky. It did not occur to her that there might be something more than this, that there were other things to be done. It did not occur to her until after she had left him, undressing in her room, sand spilling from the cuffs of her jeans, that she did not know his name.

✦　　✦　　✦

At the end of that summer she returned home from her grandparents' house to find her mother ghostly.

August. She ran to hug her and her mother pushed her away, screaming, crying, *It hurts, be careful, don't ever touch me like that!* She learned to touch her mother only from the shoulders up. Her grandparents came once a month to visit for the weekend, and on those Sunday nights, after her father had left to take them back to the city, she hid in the bathroom while her mother pounded on the door for her to come out and clean up the mess she'd made. When she finally opened the door—there was never any mess—her mother grabbed her by the hair or the back of her shirt and beat her with a long wooden spoon. This went on.

✦　　✦　　✦

Her mother is not dying, now, and Susan's car is loaded. She is ready to drive south again, a familiar route, on roads that

will take her to the town on the edge of the swamp, the bougainvillea, and a man she once imagined she loved. The phone
call had come, *Will you come back?*—flat midwestern accent
mimicking flat midwestern land.

He had not said that he loved her still; if he had, she would
have refused.

Her mother is not dying, but she has moved alone to an
apartment of square carpeted rooms and sliding glass doors.

She parks in a numbered space and climbs the steps to her
mother's door. She is carrying a grocery bag with what will
be dinner. She knocks, and her mother opens the door, re-
garding her as though they are in some other place, as though
there is water behind her, lapping. Her mother is wearing a
housedress and knee-high hose that bite her legs. She moves
aside to let her daughter in.

Her father has told Susan over and over again, *Your mother
is a good woman. She is not what you think.*

She moves in her mother's small kitchen, tearing up lettuce, steaming rice. She says, "Daddy told you I was leaving?"

"He told me."

When she leaves she will drive south through the night, ar-
riving in that town by morning. She will decide along the way
that this is the last time.

She and her mother sit across the table from one another.
Her mother's fingers are swollen, her eyes pouchy: in them
Susan sees what she has always known to be true.

"I don't think my address will be the same," she says. "I'll
have to send you the new one." And in her mother's eyes is a

multitude of children, venomous, tangled hair and naked with sticks and sharp rocks, wet sand clotted on raw pink skin. Her mother's pills are lined up by her plate like spices.

Her mother is bloated from the food she usually eats— chips and candy, milk. The apartment is spotless, the carpeting off-white, smooth pile like pavement, like skin.

She stacks dishes in the dishwasher and feels her mother slip behind her, wrap her arms around her waist and squeeze, pressing into what is still inside her, untried. The breath on the back of her neck is warm and curdled.

✦　　✦　　✦

In North Carolina she will stop for gas and coffee. She will lock her car at the pump when she goes to use the restroom. The door will have a hole by the knob where a deadbolt used to be; this will be stuffed with wet paper towels. Outside this door will be men, waiting to watch her walk back to her car.

She will walk back to her car while the men watch her, standing by their trucks. Under her windshield wiper she will find a condom, still wrapped and tucked neatly by the driver's-side door.

North Carolina, South Carolina, Georgia, her mother and her mother's children behind her, moving close to fast but not fast enough. Although she will try to focus only on where she is going, and why, and who will be waiting for her when she gets there, she will think as the interstate ribbons out behind her that she has never wanted to be farther from any place more than this one.

HERE IN THE WORLD

In the spring this is what happens: you're walking down the street and you hear it, that thing, that boy-thing— *hey, baby, baby what's your naaame*—coming out of half the cars that pass you. And you get slammed, hard, back into high school, tenth grade, when this sound was the sound of promises, of all that was good—would be good—in the world around you, of everything and everyone that was just waiting for you to walk on, swinging, slinking, because that's what high school is all about, getting ready to make your entrance. You knew it. Your hair was long and your ass was tight and you were wearing lipstick and perfume that you were sure the boys could smell from all the way over at the stoplight. The music followed you everywhere.

This is it, you thought, *I'm ready.*

This still happens, sometimes, but when it happens now you think not of your good legs or your sunglasses that hide the lines around your eyes, the ones you got this year, this long year that is just sliding from spring to summer and is not nearly done yet, you don't think of these things. You think instead of what the boys can't see, beneath your skirt, the plain white cotton underwear, no bows or lace. You think of how disappointed they would be with that. A quick kill then, a drive-by.

Hey baby, hey girl, they yell, leaning from car windows on the main drag of the peninsula, parallel with and blocks from the ocean, four lanes divided and bumper-to-bumper after dark, but not this early, not yet, not when there are hangovers to be crawled through. The ones who are out, though—they yell and whoop and beg. They are only boys.

✦   ✦   ✦

My own little boy is perfect; he has never been anything less than this. He is coming soon, to the ocean, to me, from the house where he and his father still live. The land behind that house is huge—strange to say that, that land can be *huge*—it is simply land, its own size, and it goes on. But when I lived there it was impossible for me to look out at that land without considering the reach of it, the reach of what I could not see. From our high kitchen you could step out onto a small wooden deck and face ground that sloped up gradually to a line of trees. We owned that land, those trees, and past them. We owned land I couldn't see from where I stood, acres of it, forested and dark. In the winter at dusk I would walk all the way to the trees so I could look back to my son, somewhere in our lit house, that small piece of everything.

He is coming now, or soon, and when he gets here he will

be more himself, he will have become this while I was not there to see it.

My house here is small, on a side street that runs perpendicular to the beach. There is a line of houses like mine, the same but for the colors. The neighbors' are pink and sugary green, and though in winter these houses look misplaced and faded, at this time of year there's nothing more perfect, surfaces sandy to the touch, filmed with salt and sun. Screen doors are meant to slap open in June, towels anchored by sneakers belong wet over railings.

When the three of us used to come to this house together I taught my little boy to swim, taking him into the ocean with floats on his arms, lifting him above the surf at low tide. He screamed with laughter and frantic excitement, his teeth chattering, his body slippery like an eel's while his father watched us from the shore, his eyes shaded with a graceful hand, his love for us coiled, I imagined, into a tight fearful knot below the inverted *v* of his ribcage. He was not a man at home in water and so remained always on the dry hot sand, at some distance from the foamy wash of surf—a much greater distance, it seems to me now, than I realized then.

✦   ✦   ✦

This morning I walk, like the high school girl I'm not any-more—haven't been for too long—from my house to the grocery store a few blocks up the road. The store is small and old, not like the supermarkets you'll see in shopping centers on the mainland with nonfat this and gourmet that, and the floor is always sandy, the lights along the dairy case flickering. While I stand on the sidewalk waiting for the light to change I watch the cars, the kids, the drunken sunburned babies in cutoffs holding coolers and beach chairs, bare feet mostly bleeding from bottle caps and shredded cans. They go to the store for their pretzels and skin lotion, extra-strength anything, no child-proof caps to wrestle with, and they don't care that the freezer lights are old, the cart-wheels stick and spin, the express lane is never open. These worries are for people like me, and there are very few people like me in this town.

This town, built up carelessly from summer to summer with no thought to what might last. The foundations of houses sink, the planks of the boardwalk swell and warp, awnings fly from storefronts when the winds pick up in winter. This is what happens where the land slopes under water—motion, the kind you will find only in a place where the ground on which you walk becomes smaller day by lengthening day, moving in small shifts toward disappearance.

In this town, now, at the beginning of the season that will last till Labor Day when vacations are over and school starts and heatstroke and overdoses and drownings have exhausted everyone and sent whoever is left alive back home in a line of creeping cars over the bridge—I walk through all this carrying an invisible girl, buried under the flesh of a wife, a mother, an ex-wife by September, my hand out as I cross streets with an invisible boy, little outline just so-high when I saw him last, solid body, feet right on the ground outside that big other house with his father next to him.

My perfect, perfect baby in the center of all that land—
for him I walk to the grocery store and fill my basket with
cellophaned boxes of juice, awful rods of salty cheese, eyeless
pizza goldfish, and sticky flat circles of what some would
claim is fruit, used to be fruit, might never have been fruit but
does it matter? A child is a thing to make you rethink your
idea of *food*—even dirt can be good for you, if you believe
everything you read.

✦　　✦　　✦

At fifteen you imagined your life would be—what? A movie,
a Broadway show, one production number after another, a
chorus behind you, a supporting cast, a soundtrack. You
painted your toenails while your jeans were in the dryer,
shrinking up. You would only wear them if you had to lie and
suck in to get them on and zipped—ritual, religion, girls in
bedrooms with piles of clothes around their feet, traded, dis-
carded, chosen finally with an eye to buttons and straps, the
kind that slipped off, undone.

Your body was inviolate, unfinished, and this was something that needed to be fixed.

✦　　✦　　✦

There are three boys in front of me in the checkout line. They
have two items among them, a bag of frozen French fries and
a bottle of stain remover, the kind you spray on carpets, let
sit, and vacuum up. So the third boy is superfluous, along for
moral support? Advice? His skills in comparison shopping?
The French fries are store-brand.

My own basket is filled with child-food, nothing for me. The kitchen of my house is stocked: vodka and citrus fruit.

Two of the boys are shirtless, their backs tanned, incidentally muscled the way all boys are at that age. They smell sweet, of coconut oil, sweat, and beer.

In this town, there are very few places that require shirts and shoes, and it is easy to forget the ways we have of keeping ourselves hidden.

It is some minutes before I realize that these boys are discussing the girls who are, apparently, still sleeping back in their apartment, sleeping off the secrets they have told. They speak of them in such a way that it is impossible for me to tell whether these girls are pick-ups or dates, if they have traveled any distance together, if they will last the summer out. There is no way for me to know whether the boys will return from the store to find the floors swept, the sofa-bed closed, cushions plumped, a plate of bacon waiting on the counter; or if they will return to ghosts, the smell of perfume, a hair clip, a pair of sunglasses, a note if they are lucky.

I place my items on the checkout belt.

Daiquiri, I hear, and *go-karts*.

The one with a shirt reaches into a pocket for money.

Connie's little sister, fucked up, and *phone bill*.

They jostle one another and one, a shirtless one, brushes up against me. He turns, still laughing, ready to be polite, but I can see in his amazing blue and bloodshot eyes that *polite*, for him, is only for women he does not want.

There is a small brilliant tattoo on one of his shoulders, and turning, seeing me, he hesitates.

✦　✦　✦

My husband was discreet. He never came home smelling of perfume, or damp from a late-afternoon shower, never called me by another name—nothing so vulgar as that. I, fair, never looked through his briefcase or sifted through coat pockets for receipts, for evidence. We kept a civilized distance through the winter, always a table between us, a span of couch. We carried on, waiting.

December came, with the smell of pine and cinnamon, gold-lit doorways, crystal cherubim on the mantel. My husband whispered in my ear, his hand on my head, his fingers chilled with the cold of where he'd been. It was late, past midnight and peace and goodwill, and I turned on my back, my face in the silver dark the face of an angel. Mercy, forgiveness, another child—I offered the first two for the hope of the last.

He pulled himself from me, from the deepest part of me. *Go your way and sin no more.*

My husband slept and I went down the hall to my son, picked him up with his blankets as though he were still an infant. We moved through the house, my warm son and I, him yawning against me, the lights on the tree blinking stars. It would be like freezing to death, I thought, holding him on my shoulder, the moment I let my eyes close like lying down in snow, suddenly warm and drowsy, the end of shivering, the slow dream of numbness. I stood with him at the window, the tree at my back, and watched the sky as dawn moved through it.

✦   ✦   ✦

I walk back home with the groceries and it's almost noon, late
enough by now that the day has begun in earnest for all of us.
The cars and windshields on my street reflect sun in brutal
blinding flashes; broken glass in the gutters does the same in
smaller, nastier, razor-pricks of light. The doors of houses are
open and from inside come the sounds of game shows, fights,
ringing phones and blenders.

My own house is a dark relief of swept wood floors, white
curtains, ceiling fans—what all these houses must have been,
thirty years ago or more, before the amusement park on the
boardwalk, water slides, drive-thru liquor stores and all-you-
can-eat seafood houses.

The seafood is flown in from Texas, Louisiana. Our own
bay is strained, close to exhaustion. If you listen closely to the
men in the marina you can hear the tired hopeless fury in
the way they form the word—*Louisiana*—lips stretching the
long *e* around a bitter grimace, around a place where the
water must be hot and thick, sluggish, dragging moss and
reptilian mud, nothing like our own water, salty and chill,
slightly warmer up the interior coast where the crabs are a
brilliant blue-green, and sweet.

All-you-can-eat: flown in, deep-fried, and served by blonde
girls who might well be leaving for college in the fall, for *Texas*
or *Louisiana* or some other sprawling state after a summer of
daiquiris and cuts not deep enough to scar.

I unpack my groceries, pour vodka over ice into an over-
sized plastic tumbler— translucent green, the color of car-

nival lights—and float lime slices and strawberries in it. I would raise my plastic glass to those men and their boats— good men, honorable, slow, patient—because this is the only way for them to live, through hurricanes and blizzards whose melt disrupts the bay's salinity, through chain restaurants and drunken boaters in the summer. Patient and watchful as my father was before he died, before he willed this house to me, before I came here with the thaw, thinking—wishing—I would not last till summer.

+　✦　+

You were a saint for a time, a vestal virgin. You imagined yourself in a white fluted tunic, sandaled and veiled with laurel and olive. You stood in front of full-length mirrors and worried at the reflection: those stalky legs, no matter that the other girls were jealous, too thin in your own eyes, not curved enough. Yet you cut your jeans off shorter, and shorter still, and went out like that to wait for the yells that told you you were fine, all right, the boys thought so. They looked.

You didn't understand the things that you might use your body for—ornament, adornment, this was all you knew. You charted yourself like a constellation, breasts and hips, ass and legs, stars linked by the skin between, connect-the-dots, Cassiopeia taken from the summer sky and set against the ocean.

+　✦　+

The house across the street from mine is a rental property, where families stay from Saturday to Saturday. There are four of them there now, a woman, her two little girls, her son. The woman, when I see her, will raise a hand in brief acknowledgment. She is older than me, and this, I think, is what she is most aware of. She wears yellow terry-cloth shorts and rubber sandals—vacation-clothes—and her daughters are still beautiful, brown and gold, slippery-looking, with ponytails and visors.

The boy I watch.

The horizon on the water is an illusion, the expanse of ocean level to the eye while the floor slopes away beneath it.

This mother's son walks with a cane. He grips it in his right hand and pulls that leg along after it, thin and white and braced, a metal stirrup to the shin, jointed plastic around the knee, rods up to the hem of his shorts. His arms and other leg are quick and strong. He has not been close enough for me to see his face, but I am waiting. I sit on my porch waiting.

✦   ✦   ✦

Soon the boys in cars were not enough. They passed too quickly, trailing voices and exhaust, going a block for every step of yours, a mile for every street. Their speed made you choke and panic, thinking of the time you'd lose with only legs to carry you. The years, the revolutions, clocks and seasons, stones eroding, the lapping of the ocean—you fished the boys from the water, drew them through the sand, held their heads against your belly.

You became liquid, like milk, and imagined yourself a river. They could swim in you, buoy themselves up in you, your skin gilded by the sun.

✦   ✦   ✦

On New Year's Day I sat beneath the tree, drinking spiced wine, fragile birds and berry clusters on the floor around me. I wrapped them in tissue and old towels, put them side-by-side in cartons whose corners were soft and rounded by our years of handling.

What I remember most about that day is the pale light of the sky, the snow that covered the ground with silence, the television on but muted, my son on the floor next to me sighing in and out of sleep as I filled the boxes. My husband was a shadow, pacing from the sofa to the kitchen. The morning coffee had been left on, heating to a bitter paste.

The phone rang through the afternoon, ten rings, twelve. I watched my husband, waited for him to answer, for the snow to cover our road, or stop.

The sudden quiet after a phone has stopped ringing—my husband looked at me with some surprise, his eyes dark and wide, the eyes my son would have. I stayed, under the bare tree, like a dog, a doll, and lifted the skirt off the metal tree-stand. Beneath it was a tiny box, wrapped, ribboned, a gift card on top addressed to someone else.

I remember seeing, in my husband's brief smile, the smile that would decide his good lie, the face of the boy he had been, speeding by me in an open car, that stage, those curtains, foot- and street- and taillights going on, moving fast, leaving me in their dark wake.

✦   ✦   ✦

When the boy with the cane finally comes it is dusk.

The sun does not set over the ocean here, but over the bay on the other side of the peninsula. I have wished for a place, or a day, when the sun drowned in the Atlantic, for the earth to still and reverse.

I have wished that, but this boy is crossing the street, carefully, slowly, and my son is coming soon.

The bay must be on fire now. The ocean darkens.

When the boy gets to my porch steps he stops. His pupils are wide, adjusted to the growing dark. I am sitting in a low chair, my feet and my glass on the railing, and his eyes move to my legs, the sandy calves.

"Hi," he says, and waits. "I'm James, from across the street."

My heart clenches: he speaks the sentence as a question, *street* rising in inflection up through the smells of coconut oil, seaweed, cotton candy and caramel corn from the stand at the end of the street. All this and the sounds of the midway on the boardwalk, the surf, and this boy's voice, younger than he looks, older than I thought, one hand on the head of his cane, the other on the railing of my steps.

There are so many ways for a mother's heart to break.

"Be careful, James," I say, gesturing at his hand. "I haven't sanded that railing this season. Splinters," I tell him, and reach for my glass, cover my legs with my skirt.

His color rises. He lifts his hand from the wood and looks at it as if it is something new and wonderful.

"My mother was wondering if you wanted to come for

dinner tomorrow night. She says she never sees anyone over here with you so . . ."

Here he stops. He knows that he has said too much, gone on too long. The twilight has confused him. He looks at me and sees that I am something dangerous.

"Well," I say, standing, smoothing my skirt, collecting my glass, realizing that I am going to invite this boy and his cane and his brace into my house while his mother waits, anxious, wondering where she has sent him. I am going to hold the door open for him and follow close behind and offer him water from my tap, fruit, secrets, two good legs, whatever he might want this long summer. I am going to bring him into my father's house like this. "Tell your mother thank you for me, but I can't tomorrow, James. My son is coming for a visit."

My hand is on the door, the next words in my throat—*But would you like to*—and he is gone, clattering quick down my steps and across the street like the runaway he will never be.

It is later than I thought. The days are getting longer, stretching their way toward the solstice and that shortest night, but my son will be with me for that. My little boy, little eel, his strokes through the water before he could walk—he is sleeping right now, and I have often imagined him waking, crying for me, and his father having to tell him where I have gone, what has happened to me, why I have left him.

He is sleeping in his father's house, and you would never know he belongs someplace else.

In my house I move like a mother, looking always down to

the level of my son's head, to where I think he's grown by now, watching for cords or small sharp objects that he might get to, trying to see through his bright eyes the things he would want to touch. From my kitchen window I can see the lights across the street go out, and I wonder what that boy— James—told his own mother, if he told her what I said, tried to say, if he told her I was dying, if he told her anything at all.

She will hear him if he moves at night, the heavy tread, the cane.

I make my mother-rounds, checking the burners on the stove and the locks on doors and windows—there is nothing to pick up from the floor—and arrange myself in the center of my bed, which moves in time with the low music of the ocean, that dark cradle.

+   ✦   +

You told yourself that when it ended you'd be happy, satiated and content. You pictured yourself with stories to tell, and wisdom, a laugh of a certain pitch. There would be boxes somewhere, you imagined, that you could open and when you did there would be bits and pieces, like gems, like stars, of the girl you had been, wrapped in blue sky. You pictured all this because you had to, even then. You had to believe it would end and you would still exist. Before you slept at night you closed your eyes and listened to the breathing of the girl across the room from you, in your other narrow bed, wondering how she slept while your own skin turned to ash.

+   ✦   +

In the early mornings hope comes easy. I am waking in the world, still, at home in it and my yellow house. I take my coffee to the porch, and carrying on the breeze between these houses is the smell of bacon, suntan oil, calamine lotion, baby shampoo in the steam from an open bathroom window.

Today is a day for waiting, but I am ready for this.

My husband stopped loving me sometime around the season's change, the carols, the garlands of fir and holly. How long this process, this *stopping*, took for him I have no idea, and though I might have wished to be destroyed by it, to have the hard grace to surrender—*I am over*—this is not possible. I am not, it seems, so graceful as I had thought, or as I used to be.

But I can do the little things, more of them every day, and my son is coming. His float is ready, inflated, his towel with bubbling fish; these things are by the door.

I leave my coffee on the porch and walk down the street, past the other houses, the concession stand, and up the steep dunes, heels digging in the hot sand. The early sun is warm. I am moving toward the water.